Tony asked.

"Of course I do. I'm thinking right this minute that if we hurry, I'll be home in time to watch *The Maltese Falcon* on the late show," Jerri answered.

A smile lit Tony's face. "Oh good! It's one of my favorites."

"We'll both watch it," she said, gazing into his eyes. His fingers tightened on hers, and he leaned slightly forward. His lips opened to make some affectionate comment, but she spoke before he could do so. "You in your room, and I at home in my apartment. I'll think of you," she added softly.

Tony drew a long breath and held it. "One of these days, Geraldine . . ."

JOAN SMITH

has written many Regency Romances but likes working with the greater freedom of Contemporaries. She also enjoys Mysteries and Gothics, collects Japanese porcelain, and is a passionate gardener. A native of Canada, she is the mother of three.

"Don't You Ever Think of
Anything But Business?"

Dear Reader:

I'd like to take this opportunity to thank you for all your support and encouragement of Silhouette Romances.

Many of you write in regularly, telling us what you like best about Silhouette, which authors are your favorites. This is a tremendous help to us as we strive to publish the best contemporary romances possible.

All the romances from Silhouette Books are for you, so enjoy this book and the many stories to come.

Karen Solem
Editor-in-Chief
Silhouette Books

JOAN SMITH
Tender Takeover

Silhouette *Romance*

Published by Silhouette Books New York
America's Publisher of Contemporary Romance

SILHOUETTE BOOKS,
300 E. 42nd St., New York, N.Y. 10017

Copyright © 1985 by Joan Smith
Cover artwork copyright © 1985 Corrine Winnick

Distributed by Pocket Books

All rights reserved, including the right to reproduce
this book or portions thereof in any form whatsoever.
For information address Silhouette Books,
300 E. 42nd St., New York, N.Y. 10017

ISBN: 0-373-08003-4

First Silhouette Books printing February, 1985

10 9 8 7 6 5 4 3 2 1

All of the characters in this book are fictitious. Any resem-
blance to actual persons, living or dead, is purely coincidental.

Map by Ray Lundgren

SILHOUETTE, SILHOUETTE ROMANCE and colophon are
registered trademarks of the publisher.

America's Publisher of Contemporary Romance

Printed in the U.S.A.

Books by Joan Smith

Silhouette Romance

Next Year's Blonde #234
Caprice #255
From Now On #269
Chance of a Lifetime #288
Best of Enemies #302
Trouble in Paradise #315
Future Perfect #325
Tender Takeover #343

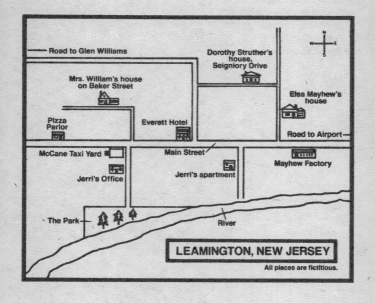

Chapter One

Jerri Tobin counted the men descending the ramp of the plane, and then counted the cars waiting. Twelve men, four cars, so unless there was a lot of sharing, she should pick up a fare. It was a calculated risk, driving to the private airport, but business was slow in Leamington on a weekday afternoon, so she'd driven her taxi out on the chance of a pickup. But now her heart sank as the men, who looked alarmingly like clones—all in dull business suits and carrying briefcases—began making a beeline for the waiting cars. Every single one of them got into one or the other of the cars.

She was about to return to her taxi in the parking lot and leave the airport, when another man appeared at the top of the ramp. This one didn't look like the others. She wondered what this sleek racehorse was doing amidst the dobbins. He was younger, taller, well built, with a muscular frame encased in a pale fawn suit. Such a well-fitting suit hadn't come off a rack, and the accessories seemed to be carefully chosen. His shirt was dark brown, his tie a creamy beige, and his handkerchief that peeped out in the top pocket of his jacket was dark brown. She noticed that his hair was dark and his face looked tanned, though it was difficult to see his features clearly.

He must be a model, Jerri decided, and wondered what a model was doing in Leamington, a rather small town in New Jersey. It didn't seem likely he was coming to be photographed at the Mayhew Machinery factory, the town's main distinction.

As she stood watching him, waiting for him to step down the stairs, he pulled out a pair of sunglasses and put them on. The afternoon sun reflected from them, obliterating his face. The simple addition of the dark glasses changed her feelings about the man. With his face disguised, she suddenly thought he might be someone famous traveling incognito. Or someone infamous for that matter. A movie star, a big-league gambler, someone wanted by the police, perhaps?

The way he hesitated at the top of the ramp, looking all around, suggested that last possibility. Or did he just enjoy standing a few feet above the rest of the world? From the proud set of his shoulders, he might have been a king surveying his domain. When he'd looked in all directions, he finally descended the ramp.

Jerri hurried forward, her interest aroused by this intriguing stranger. "Taxi, Mister?" she called as he approached the barrier that kept her from the airfield.

His head turned toward her, and the dark glasses glinted.

"Yes, thanks," he said, not surprised or grateful or anything. Possibly slightly bored. He should have been thankful to get a taxi at this out-of-the-way spot, but Jerri was so happy to have gotten a fare that she forgave him. She smiled a jaunty smile and reached for his briefcase.

"I'll carry this, but there's some luggage on the plane," he said. His voice was deep, authoritative, but smooth. A cashmere voice. It sounded like an actor's trained voice, but she knew she'd never heard it before.

"I'll get the luggage if you want to wait in the cab," she suggested, pointing to the parking lot where her taxi stood, coated in a film of dust.

"Fine," he said curtly, and turned away.

"You didn't tell me your name. For the luggage I mean," Jerri reminded him.

"The name's Lupino. There's an overnight bag and a two-suiter," he said, and walked to the cab. She looked at his retreating back, noticing the wide shoulders and the suggestion of a swagger in his stride.

"Hey, I'll need the baggage check!" she called after him.

He stopped and looked over his shoulder. "I don't have one. It's a private plane. Just tell them Lupino's luggage," he answered, and continued to walk away.

Jerri went into the terminal and had to wait ten minutes for the luggage to arrive. She didn't mind. It was air-conditioned, and they had a soft drink vending machine, which she made use of. It was thirsty work, hacking a cab. And the wait should mean a good tip, since Lupino was the cause of it. At least he looked like a good tipper, but you never could tell.

The baggage clerk gave her Lupino's luggage with no argument. Her cabbie's black peaked cap was enough identification. With the trained eye of her craft, Jerri noticed the exquisite lines of his calfskin luggage and tentatively put the name Gucci to it.

After she had returned to her cab and placed the luggage in the trunk, she hopped behind the wheel and asked over her shoulder, "Where to, Mr. Lupino?"

"The Everett Hotel," he answered.

This didn't surprise her. On those rare occasions when celebrities or politicians came to Leamington, they always put up at the Everett. It was a small, chic hostelry with a fabled dining room.

"Are you staying in town long?" Jerri asked, in the friendly but impersonal manner of cabdrivers, as she started the engine and pulled away. The sun wasn't in Mr. Lupino's eyes now, and she waited for him to take off his dark glasses so she could get a look at him in the rearview mirror. He turned to look out the window without removing the glasses.

His profile belonged on an ancient Roman coin, she thought. It reminded her of Brutus or Claudius. His thick, dark hair was ruffled from the wind. Though he wore it fairly short, it was long enough to have a slight curl, with one lock hanging over his forehead. His nose was classic, artfully chiseled and strongly sculpted. His lips were full and his chin prominent, but more than any of these details, the proud tilt of the head suggested a noble ancestry. There was a haughty arrogance in the very set of his shoulders.

"I'll only be here as long as my business takes," he answered. There was something in his tone that discouraged conversation, but it didn't discourage Jerri Tobin. She was a professional seeker of facts. Her true métier wasn't driving a cab; she was a private investigator.

"You must be in heavy machinery," she said leadingly. She didn't believe it, but it might call forth his real business.

She noticed the quick jerk of Lupino's head at this innocent statement. "A shot in the dark," she added, wondering why his lips had taken on that tense, suspicious look. "Mayhew Machinery is the only big outfit in town."

When driving permitted another quick look in the rear-view mirror, she saw that his lips had assumed their natural position. "Heavy machinery?" he asked. "No, that's not my racket."

The word "racket" conjured up quite another line of work. Didn't all the racketeers in the gangster movies wear dark shirts, light ties, and sunglasses? It was practically a uniform. She felt a moment's apprehension, and decided that discretion was the better part of valor. If Mr. Lupino had set up a discreet gambling party in his room at the Everett, it wasn't her affair.

She was silent for the next mile, but when they sped past Mayhew's factory, she pointed it out. Not that he could possibly miss it since the smokestacks were quite notice-able.

"That's the machinery factory I was talking about," she mentioned.

Mr. Lupino looked with sharp interest at the complex of buildings. Even when they were past it, he kept craning his neck around. "I don't see many cars there for the size of the factory," he commented.

"The plant's in some kind of trouble, I believe," she told him.

"What kind of trouble?"

"I'm not sure. I hear business isn't very good." she answered vaguely.

It was only one more mile into the city proper. Jerri felt dissatisfied with her passenger. She was always practicing her craft, and she had failed quite miserably to discover anything about Mr. Lupino. She didn't even know where he came from. The chartered plane had arrived from New York, but that didn't mean much. Atlantic City, the home of gambling in the state, would have been more appropriate for this man.

"It's warm today," she said idly. "If I didn't have to work, I'd hop the next charter to Atlantic City and catch the ocean breezes. Have you ever been there?"

"To the ocean? Yes, often," he replied.

"No, I meant to Atlantic City."

There was a longish silence before he answered. "No, I never have." The lips seen in her rearview mirror quivered slightly. It was hard to read them, but it looked as though Mr. Lupino was biting back a smile. This annoyed her, and she felt a pronounced wish to ruffle his calm. She toyed with the idea of hinting at his occupation, but in the interest of a good tip, she decided not to.

"For sea breezes, I prefer the Pacific to the Atlantic," he said, "and for gambling, I prefer Las Vegas."

She gave a satisfied smile that she had pegged him right as a gambler. She thought he probably spent a good deal of time at Las Vegas.

When they pulled to a stop in front of the Everett Hotel, she reached for one of the cab company's cards and handed it to Mr. Lupino. "If you need a cab while you're in town, give us a call," she said, smiling to ensure that good tip.

"I'll do that," he answered, leaning forward to take the card. With his lips close to her ear he asked quietly. "Where do you go for a good time in this joint?" His voice no longer reminded her of cashmere. It sounded like the purr of a tomcat, insinuating, and laden with sexual overtones.

Considering the tame options in Leamington, she was at a loss to inform him. "People don't usually come to Leamington for a good time," she admitted. "There's a place on Bay Street. It has a restaurant downstairs and a tavern and dancing girls above. It's called the Double Decker." Yet even as she mentioned this sleazy place, she knew it wasn't Mr. Lupino's style.

"Are they good—ah, *dancers?*" he asked, his little laugh imbuing the word with squalid overtones.

"I'm afraid I couldn't tell you, Mr. Lupino. I don't dance myself. I mean, people go there to dance as well as see the floor show, but I've never been there," she said, flustered by the nearness of his lips to her ear. He still leaned forward. She could feel his breath on her neck.

"Hmm," he said. "I thought a cabdriver would know all the hot spots."

"If you're after that kind of a good time, you've come to the wrong hotel," she told him. "It's the Leicester that . . . that . . . that would suit you better," she finished, flushing, and angry with both him and herself.

He drew his head away from her ear and said blandly, "I'll bear it in mind."

She got out, feeling a sense of escape, and opened his door. "I'll take your luggage," she said.

Mr. Lupino was already registering by the time she got the luggage inside. He still had on his sunglasses, and looked more like a racketeer than ever, wearing them indoors. He palmed a bill into her hands. "Thanks, sonny," he said, and smiled. He had very nice teeth, white and even, and probably capped, she decided.

The "sonny" surprised her. "I'm not . . ." But she was eager to see the size of the bill. Her first glance showed her its denomination, and joy made her forget her denial. "Gee, thanks, Mr. Lupino! Be sure to call us anytime you need transportation." She grinned.

"You'll be hearing from me."

A bellboy had already taken his cases. Lupino turned and walked away, taking long, sure strides toward the elevator. Jerri stuck the bill into her pocket and hurried back to her taxi.

It was four-thirty and the city was quiet. She decided to nip into her office and check the telephone answering machine to see if by a miracle someone had called while she was out. She couldn't afford a secretary. The red light indicating a message was conspicuously off. She drew a weary sigh and walked into the washroom to splash water on her face.

The sight that greeted her in the mirror wasn't exactly a surprise. Jerri had put on her cap in front of a mirror three hours ago, and knew how she looked. Funny, she hadn't felt dissatisfied with her appearance then. Why should she now?

The peaked cap was pulled low on her forehead, shadowing her eyes. With her high, broad cheekbones and strong jaw, she looked boyish. She didn't wear makeup when driving for Mike McCane, and to complete the illusion of being masculine, she always tucked her hair up under the cap. A plaid shirt and leather vest concealed her shape, and the blue jeans and tan boots were also sexless. She looked a bit like a boy, and that was fine with her. One day's driving with her long, blond hair falling free under the cap had shown her the wisdom of this disguise. It was really shocking how many men tried to hit on a female cabdriver. Of course her customers usually realized she wasn't a young man once she'd spoken a few words, but they didn't seem much interested in trying to pick her up either.

She wondered if Mr. Lupino would have made a move if he'd known she was a woman. A frisson scuttled up her spine at the memory of that purring tomcat voice in her ear. She pulled off the cap, removed three bobby pins and shook her head. A tousled cascade of pale blond hair fell to her shoulders, changing her appearance dramatically. It was her most striking feature, and suggested the soft, white glow of moonlight rather than the golden shine of the sun. The broad cheekbones that formerly looked boyish took on an intriguing new quality, hinting at the Slavic strain in her heritage. It was now clearly revealed that her cool gray eyes were wide-set, fringed with inky lashes, and topped with a fine arch of dark brows.

Her full lips were always kept closed in these self scrutinies. To open them would reveal the space between her front teeth. That fraction of an inch loomed as wide as a chasm in her mind. She hated that gap with a passion. Her sprinkling of freckles she didn't mind, since she could always cover them with makeup, but nothing short of orthodontics would help her teeth.

"Cute," her well-intentioned friends called her smile, but she didn't want to be cute. She wanted to look like Greta

Garbo, or some other cool, sophisticated, mysterious, and very dangerous lady. Someone not to trifle with, if you knew what was good for you. She knew it was childish, but everyone has illusions or fantasies.

This particular fantasy, she supposed, came from her life-long love affair with romantic mysteries. And this love affair, of course, was her father's influence. Jerri winced when she thought of her father. The pain was still sharp. He'd only been buried a week ago. Jerri ran her fingers through her hair and turned from the mirror to return to the outer office.

It wasn't a very grand office, just a room on a side street in a small New Jersey town. The tattered looks of it told her something of her father's life—a meager existence was all he had eked out of the business, but Joe had loved it, and so did she. Looking at the door leading to the hallway she read backward the words on the frosted glass panel in the top half. JOS. E. TOBIN, DISCREET PRIVATE INVESTIGATIONS. She should change it to Jerri Tobin now, since she meant to continue in her dad's business. Or maybe Jerry, to make it sound like a man. Sure, Jerry was as good as Jerri as a nickname for Geraldine.

As she sat looking at the frosted panel, a frown formed between her brows. Joe had managed a living out of the business, but now the customers didn't seem to trust a young woman. The Argus Insurance Company hadn't called since Joe's death. He'd often done jobs for them, investigating claims for stolen articles. It was just routine work, checking out pawn shops and so on, but it paid well. Joe had also managed to get a few local businesses to let him install electronic alarm and surveillance systems, but unfortunately she didn't know as much as Joe about electronics. Jerri cast a discouraged eye on the electronics text book on the desk, knowing she should get busy and learn it. "The wave of the future," Joe called it. Joe also hired himself out as a security guard upon occasion, but she wasn't big or strong enough to be a bouncer, and that was really what that job amounted to. They also traced runaway teenagers, but lately the teenagers seemed to be staying home.

So to make a living wage, Jerri drove a cab for Joe's friend, Mike McCane, while waiting for the big case, the one that would show Leamington she was as good as her father. Mike was a good contact for her line of business. The cabdrivers knew everything that was going on in town.

Jerri leaned back on the hard-backed chair in front of Joe's battered desk and sighed wearily. Her hair fell like a curtain behind her. She tilted the chair and put her booted feet on the desk to think. She'd been driving for four days, and would drive next week as well. The money would pay the month's rent on the office, but there was still her apartment rent left to pay. And then there was the five thousand in Joe's bank account, now hers, that had come as a total shock.

It had all been deposited at one time, just a week before his death. Five thousand dollars. Joe never got that much for a job. Maybe he'd won it at gambling, or in some lottery. There was nothing in the files to indicate that it had come from a customer, and he hadn't told her of any big case. Not that there could have been any such case, since Joe had spent half the month in various taverns, drinking beer. She'd begun to worry about the number of hours he spent there, but he had never seemed to be at all drunk when he returned to the office.

Maybe he'd been working on a divorce case. He told her he didn't take divorce cases, but she suspected the truth of it was that he took anything that was offered, but didn't want her involved in the messy divorce cases. He only let her work on what he called "respectable" cases. Well, he was gone now, and if the five thousand was an advance from a customer, she'd soon find out. Nobody paid out five grand without expecting the job done to his satisfaction.

While she sat thinking, the phone jangled. This was the thrilling moment. You never knew who might be on the other end of the line. It could be a robbery, a kidnapping, or a murder case!

"Tobin Private Investigations. Tobin here," she said.

"It's your aunt, Jerri," a very cultured, very annoyed voice said.

Those elegant accents called up a vivid image of Aunt Dorothy, her mother's sister. Dorothy Struthers was one of the grande dames of Leamington society. Her best friend was Elsa Mayhew, of the Mayhew Machinery Company. Between them, they ruled society with an iron fist. It was, of course, a great embarassment to Dorothy that her very own niece should be a private investigator. Talking to Jerri was the closest Dorothy would ever come to crime.

"Hi, Dorothy. What can I do for you?" Jerri asked.

"I'd like you to drop around the house when you finish work. Five, isn't it, when you close your snoop shop?" Since she couldn't talk Jerri out of her work, she made a joke of it with her friends by using this name.

Six, however, was the hour Jerri went off duty for the Empire Cab Company. "Not tonight. I'm on a case. I'll be here till six," Jerri prevaricated. Dorothy would have a fit if she ever learned her niece's new avocation.

There was a tsk of annoyance before Dorothy continued. "Six then. What are you working on? I hope it's not the McAllister divorce."

"I don't do divorce work, Dorothy. What is it you want?"

"I received a letter from your mother. I thought you might like to see it."

"Oh!" Jerri said, and felt a spurt of excitement, which soon turned to chagrin. Mom had had time to digest the fact of Joe's death, and might want Jerri to come to Europe. On the other hand, it might mean that Mom was going to get married again. "All right, Dorothy. I'll stop by at six, but I won't be staying for dinner."

"I've had the cook prepare dinner for you. There's no one else coming, if that's what's worrying you. You won't be exposed to anyone respectable," Dorothy added irascibly.

It was less the respectable guests, otherwise known as bores, than the food that kept Jerri away. Aunt Dorothy was so determined to be thin that she never served anything but rabbit food—plates of cold vegetables with unappetizing sauces. Ugh! Jerri was a devotee of fast foods: pizza, tacos, submarine sandwiches, and the delicious hamburgers they never made quite right in Europe. The world of fast food had come as a revelation to her when she moved permanently to America.

"I have a date at seven," Jerri said, carefully crossing her fingers, and not adding that the date was with the cook at the Mexican Delight, which served the best burritos in town.

"With whom?" Dorothy asked swiftly, and with a touch of suspicion.

"Nobody you'd know, Dorothy. I have to go now. See you around six. *Ciao*." Jerri hung up, left the office, and went back to her cab. It was nearly five, and there'd be a few pickups from the stores and offices downtown.

She had half a dozen customers between five and six o'clock, all local. At six she drove the cab into the yard and handed in her receipts.

"You had a call, Jerri," Mike told her. "A guy at the Everett wants you to pick him up tomorrow at ten. He wants to book the cab for a couple of hours. He asked especially for you," Mike added, casting a knowing look at her.

Jerri's eyes were bright and curious, and on her cheeks two flags of red revealed her interest. "He asked for me?" she inquired. "How did he know my name? I didn't tell him."

"He didn't ask by name. Just for the driver who'd picked him up at the airport. I guess he was impressed with your driving," Mike added, laughing.

"I guess he was," she agreed, refusing to rise to Mike's bait.

"How's your other business going these days?" Mike asked, with more sympathy than interest.

"Fine, Mike. Just fine," she said firmly. None of them thought she could do Joe's job, but she could, and she'd show them all one of these days.

"Go on," Mike said, pushing a gray fedora back on his head and narrowing his blue Irish eyes at her. "Why don't you can it? That's no job for a lady like you. All that fancy schooling in Europe and all. You should get married and settle down. I don't know how many times your Dad said so.''

"I know. I know. I'm only a woman, fit to wield a mop and broom. Thanks anyway. See you tomorrow, Mike.''

After Jerri tossed her cap on the desk and sauntered out, she got into her father's battered Ford. It was a plain dark blue model, six years old. Joe had driven it because he claimed it was inconspicuous for tailing people. She drove it to Seigniory Drive, where it stood out quite remarkably amidst the Mercedeses and Lincolns parked in the driveways.

The cabbies called Seigniory Drive "Rich Row." The houses here were large and beautiful. In late May, the bushes and fruit trees were in bloom, and the trees were newly leafed, giving them a gentle, fresh look. Dorothy Struthers lived in a brick Georgian house with small pillars and a white door with a fanlight at the top.

She sat awaiting her niece in the living room, a stately chamber that looked as if it had escaped from a decorating magazine. No ashes marred the ashtrays, the magazines looked untouched, and the chocolate wafers formed an unbroken pattern in their crystal dish.

Dorothy was a part of the decor. She had dressed for dinner in a long blue gown that clung to her meager curves and showed off her slight figure. Her face was broad and made up to perfection, but too thin. She reminded Jerri of a pale shadow of her own mother. The two women had the same Slavic features, but in Dorothy everything had faded. Slavic faces didn't take too well to starvation. Dorothy's large bones should have some flesh on them. Her natural exuberance had also been toned down to a sophisticated languor.

"Oh, there you are," Dorothy said, her eyes gliding with distaste over the leather vest and jeans. "What have you been doing in that outfit, Jerri, rustling cattle?"

"Working. May I see Mom's letter please?"

"Wouldn't a business suit be more suitable for the office?" her aunt objected.

"I wasn't in the office much today. I was out on business most of the time," Jerri told her.

A pained expression pinched Dorothy's face. "I wish you'd reconsider this private investigating thing you've gotten yourself into, dear," she urged. "It's not at all suitable for a lady of your background."

"It *is* my background. I'm just continuing in the family business. What's wrong with that?" Jerri asked reasonably.

"You know perfectly well what's wrong with it!" her aunt snapped back. "That your mother made the dreadful mistake of marrying Joe Tobin, doesn't constitute your background. Marie only lived with him for eleven months. It's all my fault she ever married him. If I hadn't invited her for a visit to Leamington that summer, and if she hadn't misplaced her diamond bracelet, she'd never have met such a person as Tobin."

"And I wouldn't exist to be an embarrassment to you," Jerri finished. Then she added impishly, "But Dad found her bracelet, didn't he, Dorothy? Imagine one of your fancy guests nabbing it!"

"The whole thing was an unfortunate misunderstanding, and I do *not* regret your existence, my dear, only the manner in which you choose to waste it. You're a bright and attractive woman, Jerri. You've had the best education, as well as that expensive finishing school in Switzerland when

Marie was married to Count Fragliani. The daughter of a countess should not be playing as a private detective.''

"I'm not playing," Jerri countered mildly. "And Mom isn't a countess any longer either, since the divorce. She's using her maiden name at the moment, I believe. Marie Sobieski."

"That's not a name to trifle with either!" Dorothy objected, swift to defend her own maiden name. "The Sobieskis are an excellent old aristocratic family. Actually Marie is getting married again. That's what the letter is all about. She wants you to go and live with her and Charles d'Anjou in Paris. Charles is a *very* influential gentleman in the world of journalism. Oh, you're so lucky!" Dorothy said, clapping her hands to indicate the marvelous opportunity.

Jerri listened to this stunning news with no sign of enthusiasm. She was happy her mother had found someone new to love, and hoped very much that this marriage would last. But she'd learned from hard experience that her place in these brief marriages was uncertain. She was a novelty for a month or so, till her mother wanted to go off on some holiday, at which time Jerri had been put into the most convenient school. It had been that way for as long as she could remember. Brief bouts of being loved and cherished and pampered, followed by long periods of isolation.

It was for that reason she had decided to come to America when she turned twenty-one and try to make a home with her father. That hadn't been wildly successful either. She and Joe Tobin had been total strangers, coming from completely different backgrounds. Joe lived in a small apartment, which meant she had to rent an apartment for herself. But in spite of the difficulties, she'd come to know and love him. He was always there, at least. She felt that he enjoyed having her with him in his business, even if he did feel obliged to tell her it was unsusitable.

"May I see the letter?" Jerri asked again, and finally her aunt handed it over.

It contained many references to herself. Marie was worried about her daughter and inquired if Geraldine was all right, and if she was meeting any "interesting" young men, which meant rich men. Marie also said she'd be writing to Geraldine soon, but she might forget to do it with the wedding to plan. She urged both Dorothy and Geraldine to attend the wedding, but didn't remember to mention the date—just like Mom!

"I'm happy for her," Jerri said. "Are you going to the wedding?"

"I couldn't possibly get away in this season, with all the clubs opening and the charity ball to plan, but you must certainly go. You'll notice on the second page she says she hopes you'll make your home with her and Charles. If you're smart, Jerri, you'll accept her offer," Dorothy said, nodding wisely. "I don't feel comfortable seeing you take over Tobin's work. He dealt with some very seedy clients, I can tell you. God only knows what kind of people you're meeting there," she added, genuinely worried.

Jerri took her aunt's hand and squeezed it. "I *do* appreciate your concern, Dorothy, but you don't have to worry. I can take care of myself. It's about time I started, don't you think? I don't want to be shuttling around Europe for the rest of my life. I want to settle down. I don't feel I belong anywhere." She held the letter, reluctant to return it. It was nice to hold on to something tangible from her mother. For during the periods they were together, they were the best of friends. They'd always had such wonderful times with each other, which made going to the various schools all the more difficult to bear.

"You're welcome to make your home with me. I've asked you a dozen times," her aunt reminded her.

It was true, but the formality of life with Dorothy didn't suit Jerri. She wanted to be independent. "I appreciate it, Dorothy, but it's enough just knowing you're here, close by if I need you," she said.

This discussion was old territory for them both, and soon forgotten. "You can keep Marie's letter if you like. It's got the address so you can write to her. You'll be going to the wedding, at least?" Dorothy asked.

"I'll think about it," Jerri answered doubtfully. Mostly she thought she couldn't afford the trip. She had the five thousand, but there was some possibility it might have to be returned to the customer if Joe hadn't done the job. The only person she'd know at the wedding would be her mother, and they wouldn't have much time together. Then, too, Mom would be going away on her honeymoon as soon as the wedding was over. A visit later on, after she had settled in with Charles, seemed more sensible.

"Let me know. Keep in touch, Jerri," her aunt urged. "Oh, by the way, Elsa Mayhew wants you to come to her party tomorrow evening. It's her big do of the year, so everybody will be there. It's time you began meeting some of the right sort of people, my dear. You're not likely to find any clients, but you might just meet some eligible young man. *Do* come. Lawrence and I will pick up up. Seven-thirtyish?"

Jerri appreciated her aunt's concern. Even though the

party would be a dead bore, with everyone except herself over forty, possibly one of the guests would have a son her age. It was time she began meeting some nice men, and it was certainly true she didn't meet them at her work.

"Thanks. That sounds great. How formal is it?"

"Not formal. I'm wearing a long skirt since Elsa always does, but a short dress will be fine, as long as it's fancy. No slacks, dear," she added, glancing at Jerri's jeans.

"Okay, I'll be ready. How is Elsa anyway? I drove past the plant today, and noticed there weren't many cars in the parking lot. What's going on?"

"It seems they've lost contracts and had to lay off quite a few workers. There's some sort of technical problem. Ever since Bill Dallyn, her chief engineer, retired, Elsa's been plagued with troubles, poor woman. And of course it had to happen after her husband died. Elsa hasn't a notion how to run a company. She's talking about selling it," Dorothy mentioned.

"That might be the best thing."

"She could always get married again and let her husband handle it, but she doesn't have any prospects at the moment. However, we shan't discuss all these unpleasantries tomorrow evening. I believe Elsa's having the party to forget her troubles."

"I won't say a word. Well, I better be going now. Thanks for the letter, Dorothy." Jerri kissed her aunt's cheek and left.

Chapter Two

When Jerri awoke in her apartment the next morning, her mother's letter sat on the bedside table where she'd left it the night before. She'd tried to phone her mother, but hadn't reached her. She'd wanted to arrange a visit for some time after the honeymoon, but unless she discovered the truth about that mysterious five thousand dollars, she really couldn't afford to go at all.

Money was a constant worry, and worrying about money reminded her of her morning's work—not in her office, but driving the taxi for Mr. Lupino. The memory of him was with her as she showered and shrugged into her housecoat for breakfast. She was pleasantly excited at the prospect of seeing him again. Maybe she'd find out a little more about him today, what his occupation was, for instance. He'd said he was in Leamington on business, but if it was arranging a gambling session in his room, he wouldn't need a taxi. Why didn't he rent a car and drive himself for that matter? The man was a mystery, and she *did* love a mystery.

Jerri padded into her tiny kitchen and reached for the cereal box. She delighted in the variety of cereals she found in the supermarkets in the States. All kinds of delicious, crunchy ones with bits of fruit and nuts and wonderful tastes. Such a treat after the porridge served in English boarding schools. As a concession to her nutritional needs, she also poured a glass of orange juice and drank it as a penance before enjoying the sugar-coated cereal.

She automatically reached for her jeans when she went into the bedroom to dress, but her hand stopped just an inch short of them. Maybe she wouldn't wear her jeans today. There was no reason she had to wear them whenever she drove for Mike. She'd wear her beige flannel slacks instead, and the dark green silk shirt Mom had given her before she came to the States. She always wore her gold chain with the ankh symbol with that shirt, and she fastened it around her neck.

When she was dressed, she realized that what she had put on to chauffeur Mr. Lupino was her best casual outfit. "Who are you trying to impress, dummy?" she asked herself, and laughed. But everyone kept telling her it was time she met some nice young man. Lupino was young, and very much a man. Just how "nice" he was was debatable, but this might be her opportunity to find out.

Jerri brushed her pale blond hair out till it shone in loose waves around her collar. It framed her face like a living, moving golden frame. The cap would look out of place with this outfit, but what the heck. She could take it off once they were driving. She'd wear it when she went to pick him up at the Everett so that he'd recognize her. As she spread a concealing cream over her freckles, she realized that what she was setting out to do was knock Mr. Lupino dead with shock. Sonny indeed! Had he really mistaken her for a young man? She didn't believe it for a minute. He'd just been teasing her, but he wouldn't have said it if she hadn't appeared unfeminine. Today he'd see she could look like a woman when she chose to. She ran her eyes down her shapely body with satisfaction, then turned her attention to her face again.

She spread a soft pink gloss over her lips and discreetly accentuated the outline of her eyes with a kohl pencil. The result was entirely satisfactory, till she smiled and became aware of the gap between her front teeth. "Damn," she muttered, and picked up her purse to leave.

Jerri stopped at her office to check her telephone messages—none, of course. She wrote a sign for the door, "Back at two," and taped it on the frosted window. Not that anyone would come, she thought dejectedly. She really must get cracking on that electronics book and learn about the "wave of the future." Again the five thousand dollars popped into her mind, and she wondered how she could discover where it came from. The office files hadn't been at all helpful, and Mike McCane had no idea.

She parked her car at the taxi stand, slammed the door shut behind her, and picked up her cap in the office.

"Hi, Jerri," Mike said. "Lupino's hired the cab at a flat rate of twenty-five bucks an hour. Just take him where he wants to go, and don't bother with the meter."

"I wonder why he didn't rent a car," she said, frowning.

"Maybe he lost his license." Mike guessed.

Somehow that explanation seemed entirely feasible. She

could easily picture Mr. Lupino driving faster than the law allowed. "I wouldn't be surprised," she said, setting her cap on her head and slanting it rakishly over her right eye.

"How come you're all dressed up today? Lupino must be a looker," Mike said slyly.

"I'll be spending the afternoon in my office with a client, and don't want to have to change," she explained, but she couldn't meet Mike's eyes as she said it. She hurried away before he could inquire about the imaginary client.

Jerri arrived at the Everett Hotel at two minutes to ten. Mr. Lupino was already waiting at the door, briefcase in hand. He'd adopted a more casual style today. Under his tan suede jacket he wore an open-necked sports shirt, still managing to look fashionable. She felt a twinge of annoyance that the dark glasses were already in place. She was extremely curious to see what Mr. Lupino looked like without them.

She hopped out and held the back door open for him. "Good morning, Mr. Lupino," she said cheerfully.

He gave her a long, considering look before he smiled, a flash of white teeth showing in the sunlight.

"Good morning. For two bits an hour, I think I deserve the front seat," he said, and opened the front door to let himself in.

She leaped on this revealing speech. Who but a racketeer would call twenty-five dollars two bits? She regretted that she hadn't worn her old jeans, but as long as Lupino behaved himself, she'd be polite.

"Where to, sir?" she asked crisply as she slid behind the wheel.

Mr. Lupino had already rolled down his window and made himself at home. He was extracting a narrow cigarillo from a gold case and cutting the end. "Do you mind?" he asked.

"Not at all." It reminded her of Joe, who was seldom without a cigar between his teeth. He thought it made him look tough. "Where to, Mr. Lupino?" she repeated.

"Just drive out toward the airport for now," he said, fingering his lighter. After he had lit the thin cigar and she moved into the traffic, he continued. "Let's set a few ground rules before we go any further, shall we? My name's Tony, and I'm more comfortable with that than 'sir.'"

"That's okay with me, Tony," she answered with polite indifference.

"I presume you're blessed with a name as well," he said.

"Tobin. Jerri Tobin," she told him.

His head swiveled swiftly in her direction. From the corner of her eye, she could see the sun glint on his glasses. "Tobin!" he exclaimed.

"You might as well call me Jerri," she said, "since you don't seem to like Tobin for a name."

"I have nothing against it. It's just that you don't look Irish."

"I'm half American-Irish, with a lot of other strains thrown in," she said vaguely.

"Some Slavic blood included, if I'm not mistaken?" Tony asked, still examining her. "Those cheekbones don't come from Ireland."

"My mother is from Poland," she said.

"The Jerri, I gather, is from your father's side, short for Geraldine."

"That's right." She nodded, content to follow this harmless line of conversation.

"And do you use a boy's nickname to help your masculine disguise along?" he asked. A lazy smile was on his lips.

"I don't seem to need any help. You called me sonny before you knew my nickname," she reminded him. As they drove toward the edge of town, the traffic lessened and she was able to spare a glance at her passenger.

"I was teasing you," he said. "I'm not blind, after all."

"I thought maybe you were, since you hide behind dark glasses. But then of course you don't carry a white cane," she said idly.

"I'm not hiding. My eyes are sensitive to light."

"You must have had a successful night at the Double Decker," she answered pertly. She realized she was being more personal than she should be with a fare, and told herself to draw in the reins.

"It doesn't do to judge acquaintances too hastily, Geraldine. If you think the Double Decker, with the worst booze in town, and half a dozen dancers well past their prime, is my idea of a howling night, you misjudge me. I wasn't there more than five minutes."

"What spot did you find? I like to know these things for the benefit of my out-of-town customers," she explained.

Tony slowly blew a cloud of smoke out the window before turning back to her. "I returned to my hotel after one drink. It's dull, but at least there's no fear of poisoning or a police raid. There must be some spot between those two extremes in a city this size," he said hopefully.

"There must be, but to tell the truth, I'm not very well informed about this city's entertainment."

A pair of elegant eyebrows showed above Tony's glasses. "I would have thought an attractive young woman like you would be out every night. In fact, I regretted I hadn't asked you to join me, after I let you get away yesterday. But then you *did* mention your lack of interest in dancing," he added blandly.

She was gratified at first that he had been interested, but as she thought about it, it wasn't flattering that he might want to pick her up. "I'm quite busy in the evenings actually," she said.

"Doing what?" he asked at once.

"It doesn't seem to have occurred to you that I might be married," she replied.

"On the contrary, it was the first thing that occurred to me. I noticed yesterday you don't wear either a wedding ring or an engagement ring. I am rather observant," he admitted modestly. "The fact was verified today when you said you still use your father's name, Tobin. Since you don't have a husband to rush home to, we are still left to wonder what you do at night," he pointed out.

"I'm studying, taking some courses," she said, with a dull thought of the electronics book.

"You have some other career in mind than driving a cab then," he concluded.

"Yes," she said, but didn't expand on it.

Undismayed, he forged on with his unhelpful conversational partner. "Do I have to guess? Let me see . . ." As if to see her better, he finally removed the dark glasses and studied her profile, while she looked ahead, feigning a lack of interest, though she was completely aware of his scrutiny.

When the silence could no longer be borne, she turned impatiently to him. "Well?" she asked sharply. Even that brief glimpse was a mistake. His eyes were quite simply irresistible. A deep, dark, molten chocolate color you could drown in. They weren't the sultry, torrid eyes, she'd been imagining; they had a spark of mischief glittering in them.

"Too short tempered for a nurse or any occupation that entails much sympathetic dealing with the public. A police-woman, perhaps?" he suggested playfully. "Detective Tobin has a good ring to it. Sounds like one of New York's finest."

A surprised frown creased her brow because he had hit so close to home in calling her Detective Tobin. Of course he meant a police detective, but it was still curious. "Why do you say that?" she asked.

"I believe I mentioned your brusque manner, didn't I? Then there's your love of disguise as well. That suggests some sort of undercover dealings. Don't tell me I've guessed it in one shot!" he exclaimed, and laughed.

"No, I'm not the least interested in being a police-woman."

"An aspiring model? An actress? Some career to opti-mize your . . . assets," he said, choosing the last word carefully.

Jerri disliked the tone of this talk. She didn't want him detailing her assets. That might lead to trouble. "Something like that," she said, and immediately changed the subject. "Do you want to go all the way to the airport?" The Mayhew plant loomed up ahead, and not far beyond it was the airport.

"No, you can turn around at that factory and go back to town."

"Where in town do you have in mind?"

"Just drive along Main Street and keep going," he answered carelessly.

She remembered Mike's telling her Lupino had asked expecially for her as his driver. As he didn't appear to have any destination in mind, it was impossible not to wonder if this was his novel way of getting a date with her.

She executed a turn at Mayhew and headed back to town. "Is this how you plan to spend the whole morning?" she asked.

"Oh, no, I thought we'd find a nice quiet spot somewhere and park. Just talk a little, get to know each other. I see on the map there's a river running through Leamington. There must be something of interest to see at the waterfront," he said, and leaned his arm along the back of the seat.

"You're paying twenty-five dollars an hour to sit and talk and look at a statue?" she asked, turning to stare at him in consternation.

Tony looked utterly bored as he took another puff of his cigarillo. Any notion that he was interested in her faded, leaving total confusion behind. "Unless you have some more diverting pastime to suggest," was his ambiguous answer.

"It's your dollar. If you want to talk, it's all right with me. I certainly have nothing livelier to suggest to a total stranger," she replied. She was a little concerned about his hand, whose fingers weren't two inches from her neck, but he didn't make any move to touch her.

"Ceasing to be total strangers will be enough for today," he decided. "We don't want to rush things."

The silence that followed stretched uncomfortably while Jerri tried to decide how to handle this suggestive remark. "How long are you staying in town, Tony?" she asked, to break the silence.

"Till my business is successfuly finished, as I believe I mentioned yesterday."

"You didn't say what your business is," she said leadingly.

"No, I didn't, did I? And you didn't say what career it is that you're studying for. We'll have plenty to talk about. Where are you from, Jerri? Since you don't know the hot spots of Leamington, I imagine it's not your home town. I think I detect a hint of an accent in your speech as well."

"I don't have an accent!" she said with some force. She was very proud of her American speech. "In Europe people always know immediately that I'm an American," she said proudly.

"I see. In what part of Europe do they always know this?" he asked, his lips twitching in a smile. "I imagine it's in whatever country you were raised. England, was it?"

"I went to school there," she admitted reluctantly. "But I spent most of my holidays in the States, unless my mother made other plans. Sometimes we traveled."

"Are you familiar with Italy at all?" he asked, finally falling into an ordinary conversational manner.

"Yes, I spent some time in Rome," she replied, remembering the halcyon days of Count Fragliani.

"My own ancestors are from Naples."

"I know. I mean I knew the name was Italian, and you have a Latin look," she said.

"My mother would be horrified to hear you say so. She's Irish-American, like your father. What we are, you and I, is a pair of mongrels, like most Americans," he decided.

They entered the city, and Jerri began figuring the fastest route to the water front.

She was surprised when Tony began giving her directions. "I want you to take the road north out of town. You turn right at the traffic light," he said.

She felt the hair on her neck rise with fright. Mike had frequently warned her of the dangers of driving strange men around, but till that moment she'd thought it was foolishness. She was suddenly afraid that Tony wanted to get her alone, and was suggesting this out-of-the-way spot for that purpose.

She moistened her lips and tried to think of some reasonable way of putting him off. "The river is south, not north," she said.

"That's for later. The river won't run away, but the man I have to meet might."

She noticed then that he had taken out a little hand-drawn map and was studying it. "There should be a gas station and corner store about a mile north of town. You take a left there, and go two miles farther," he said.

She was relieved that he did actually have a destination in mind, and tried to remember what was at the place he mentioned. "That'd be past the village of Glen Williams," she told him.

"Right on the edge of it. I'm looking for a stone house by the water. It shouldn't be hard to find. There's an old Gothic church next door."

She nodded and took the proper turn. "I know the place."

The countryside was pretty in springtime, with the azure sky a backdrop to the young leaves. White angora clouds calmly sailed along, and birds warbled from the treetops, but while Mr. Lupino seemed to be enchanted by it, Jerri had something else on her mind. Why would a man like Tony Lupino be going to Glen Williams, a mere dot on the map, to do his business? Was this quiet spot being chosen to set up some wild gambling game? Why take the risk, when gambling was legal in Atlantic City? Maybe it was worse than gambling. Half a dozen horrifying alternatives sprang to mind with wicked ease.

To nudge her partner into speech, she said casually, "There's not much business that I know of in Glen Williams except fishing."

"The man I'm going to see is retired, actually. I just want to consult with him on something."

Jerri wanted to ask more questions, but felt it would be useless. The very vagueness of his answer told her of his unwillingness to confide in her. And maybe it was just as well she didn't know too precisely what he was up to.

Mr. Lupino had fallen silent. His cigarillo had gone out, and she thought he had forgotten her presence entirely. Before long they reached Glen Williams and drove through the village, with its scattering of small shops and businesses. The church was at the far edge of town, and next to it was the stone house he'd mentioned. Jerri pulled to a stop and got out to open Tony's door.

"Have you any idea how long you'll be?" she asked. "I mean if it's going to take an hour or so, I'd go and have a Coke."

"Go ahead, but I won't need quite an hour. Come back around eleven-fifteen." He picked up his briefcase and got out.

"Okay." She tipped her hat, waiting for him to leave.

Tony reached out and removed the cap from her head. "I gave up the sunglasses to let you admire my beautiful eyes. Don't you think you could get rid of the cap and let me see your hair?" he asked, his tone reasonable, though his eyes revealed his admiration as they lingered on her hair, now moving slightly in the breeze.

He smiled as he reached for her cap, holding it higher, beyond her grasp. But she refused to oblige him by playing that game. "Why do you do this job anyway?" he asked.

"I like the uniform."

"Well I don't," he said, and with a chuckle he tossed the cap through the window onto the seat of the car.

Jerri didn't drive away till he'd been admitted to the house. She turned back to Glen Williams, and kept an eye out for a coffee shop to while away the time. She parked in front of a small restaurant called Mary's Place and went in. A sprinkling of customers occupied a few of the tables. She slid onto a stool at the counter and ordered a Coke. Its sharp, cool tingling felt good against her dry throat. The woman behind the counter appeared to be in a talkative mood.

"A nice day," she said. "You must be passing through. I guess I know just about all the three hundred and forty-four people in the village."

"I just drove a friend here," Jerri answered, and decided to see if she could learn who it was that Tony was visiting. "Actually I drive a cab; that's it out front. My passenger's gone to that little house by the church. He didn't say who he was visiting." She smiled and waited hopefully for elucidation.

"He must be from the Mayhew factory in Leamington," the woman said, nodding. "That's old Bill Dallyn's place. He used to be a big chief of some kind at Mayhew before he retired."

The name jarred her memory, and aroused a host of questions. Why was Tony going to see the ex-chief engineer of the Mayhew Machinery Company? Was it just a coincidence? Tony hadn't mentioned it when she pointed out the Mayhew plant, and they'd even talked about the company a little.

"What does Dallyn do now?" Jerri asked, trying not to sound too eager.

"Nothing much. He's got a little place in Florida he goes to in the winter, but he always comes back here for the duck hunting and fishing in the spring and summer. His nephew, is it, who's visiting him? Young Ted Dallyn?"

"No, it's just a friend," Jerri said.

One of the customers at a table called to the waitress for coffee, and Jerri sat ruminating on what she'd learned. She couldn't make any sense of it. Tony had denied explicitly that his business had anything to do with heavy machinery. And besides, Dallyn was retired. But she couldn't quite put to rest the fact that she knew Mayhew was in trouble. There were articles about it in the paper every few days. It was a concern locally since Mayhew was one of the largest employers in the city.

Maybe she'd learn something at Elsa Mayhew's party that evening. It gave some point to her going, and now she looked forward to it with more interest.

Jerri finished her drink and walked through the village, stopping in a general store where she bought a bag of chips. Chips were another thing she loved about American food. They called them crisps in England, but they didn't have the variety of flavors. The vinegar ones she ate from the foil bag were delicious and tangy.

When she had finished, it still wasn't time to pick up Tony, so she waited in the car, thinking. She was making a mountain out of a molehill, she told herself sternly. Since she'd gone to work for her father, she looked for crime and double-dealing at every turn. What illegal business could Tony possibly be up to, visiting the retired chief engineer of Mayhew? The troubles, Dorothy had said, only began after Dallyn left, so obviously Dallyn had nothing to do with them. How Tony could be involved wasn't clear, but it might have something to do with Mayhew's being Tony's competitor.

But Tony wasn't in the heavy machinery "racket," to use his word, so that couldn't be it. Unless he had lied to her when she'd asked him. But why would he lie to a perfect stranger? Maybe the meeting had nothing to do with Mayhew at all. A retired chief engineer might easily have some personal business concerns. Maybe he and Tony were discussing the buying or selling of some property. Sure, that was it, she thought, and felt peaceful.

It didn't take her five minutes to figure out why she felt so peaceful. It was because she managed to come up with a plausible explanation for Tony's meeting. Boy, this job was getting to her. Next she'd be thinking her own father had been involved in it. That five thousand still wasn't explained.

Chapter Three

Jerri waited till nearly eleven-thirty in Dallyn's driveway before Tony came out of the house, still carrying his briefcase. Would he need a briefcase to transact such a simple business deal as buying or selling a property? She remembered that he never let that case out of his hand. He hadn't let her carry it at the airport. Her feeling of peace evaporated.

She got out and held the door for him, the front door this time. Tony stood a moment before getting into the car. There was a small smile of amusement on his lips, and laughter danced in his eyes. "You spoil me," he said. "Maybe I should get myself a female chauffeur. I feel positively decadent receiving such service from a woman."

"Just think of me as a man," she suggested.

"Easier said than done, but I'll *try*, Mr. Tobin," he replied, and got into the taxi.

"Do you want to go back to Leamington now?" Jerri asked when she was behind the wheel.

"It's nearly noon. I thought we might stop for some lunch, but I doubt if there's a decent restaurant here in Glen Williams," he answered.

"Why don't I drop you at a restaurant in Leamington and take the cab back to the stand? It'll be cheaper for you," she explained.

"But that leaves me without a partner for lunch!" he pointed out. "You've already told me you don't know the night spots in town, but I'm sure that even a struggling scholar *cum* taxi driver must eat out occasionally. Where do you recommend?"

She pulled the car out on to the road and headed back to the city. "I usually go to a fast-food burger or Mexican place. They have great burritos at the Mexican Delight," she said, thinking this would discourage him.

Tony turned slowly in his seat and stared at her. "To look at you, one would never suspect that you have a cast-iron stomach. That must come from your Polish side. If it were Irish, I'd have it, too."

"I forgot you're Italian! I should have recommended the Pizza Parlor," she exclaimed. Already her gastric juices were activated just thinking of the wonderful pizzas, with succulent mushrooms, cheese, and spicy pepperoni.

"Isn't there anything but fast food in Leamington?" Tony objected. "Actually the hotel has an excellent dining room, to judge by last night's dinner."

"It takes hours to eat in those fancy places," she said, her frown showing her lack of interest.

"Are we in a hurry? I find *dining* to be one of life's little pleasures. *Eating*, on the other hand, is only a primitive necessity. Fast food is like making love with your boots on,'' he added provocatively.

Unable to think of a comeback, Jerri ignored the last part of his speech. ''I'll take you wherever you want to go, Tony, and pick you up after if you want to hire the cab for part of the afternoon, too, but I don't care to dine with you.'' Her fears were aroused by that casual mention of making love. There was a sensual quality to this man that frightened her.

''All right, you win,'' he said, surprising her by his easy capitulation. ''We eat, not dine. I leave our gastronomic fate to your discretion, with the single exception of burritos. I've tried them—dog food in a leather pouch. Neither a hamburger nor a pizza will kill me, but a burrito may very well do the trick.''

He'd misinterpreted her remark to mean she'd eat with him, but since he couldn't do much harm to her psyche in the twenty minutes or so the lunch would take, she let him get away with it. She decided, however, to teach him a lesson and make this meal an experience he wouldn't care to repeat. She took him to the Pizza Parlor, the loudest, busiest eatery in town. Customers had to line up for a ticket before placing their orders, and go and pick up the food when it was ready. The food was good and the price was right, so there would be a full house at noon. With luck, they might even have to stand in a long line and wait.

A barrage of noise made up of music, human voices, and electronic buzzers struck their ears as they entered the place. Jerri was a little disappointed to see the noon crowd hadn't arrived in full force yet, so that a few tables were free.

"A charming spot," Tony said, leveling an accusing eye at her. She ignored it and pointed to an empty table. On the way to it, she took a plastic ticket bearing the number seventeen.

The tables were spaced close together, so that even sitting down was inconvenient. "Do you want a beer with your pizza?" she asked nonchalantly.

"I do, but I don't want you to drink when you're driving," he said.

"Oh I don't want one. I'm a Coke-aholic," she answered cheerfully, pleased to note that he wasn't happy with the place. His expression became somewhat grim when arrivals at the next table jarred his shoulder.

"They're a little short-staffed here," he said a moment later.

"This is a cafeteria. When your number is called, you have to go up to the counter to order your food, and get it when it's ready."

"That will take care of our exercise," he said through thin lips.

Over the loudspeaker a whining voice called out, "Order seventeen. Order seventeen."

"That's us!" Jerri said, showing him the card.

"There's nothing like the homey bellow of loudspeakers and the shuffle of paper plates to whet the appetite. I'll place the order."

He began to rise, but she hopped up before him. "You're my customer. Let me do it," she said.

"Whatever happened to the customer always being right?" he asked.

"It went the way of the dodo, along with corsets and

wood stoves.'' With a little laugh, she went to the counter and ordered a pizza that would be sure to set fire to her customer's throat. Plenty of hot chili and the spiciest pepperoni, along with a liberal dose of anchovies. Then she went to the wet bar and got him a draft of beer and her own Coke.

''This looks appetizing at least,'' he said, when she returned to the table. ''Cheers!'' He lifted the frosty glass and drank.

''Skol!'' she replied, raising her glass in salute. The sparkling drink felt like fireworks as it went down, tingling against her throat as the bubbles exploded. ''The day they invented this stuff, they lost a lot of wine customers,'' she said contentedly.

A reluctant smile took possession of Tony's face as he observed her. When he spoke, his voice conveyed approval. ''It's a pleasant change to meet a woman with simple tastes. I imagine you prefer rhinestones to diamonds, too, and denim to silk and satin.'' His liquid eyes traveled slowly over her face as he spoke, causing a little uneasiness to stir in her. ''It's strange, you know, that you have a continental, sophisticated appearance when you're not impersonating a boy, yet you seem violently opposed to any suggestion of luxury.''

Jerri didn't make any reply for a moment. Her face assumed a contemplative expression as she considered the tumultuous life her mother led in her search of riches and entertainment. ''According to Lao-tse, the old Chinese philosopher, 'There is no calamity greater than lavish desires.' I believe that. I've seen the disastrous consequences of hankering after luxuries.''

Tony studied her closely, with a question in his eyes. "You're too young for such a philosophy, Jerri. What's wrong with wanting some of the good things in life? It's the American dream, and you seem proud of your American blood."

"It's not the *real* American dream," she objected. "Maybe what I mean is diamonds and silks and satins aren't really the good things in life. What pleasure can anyone get from wearing a chip of cold carbon on their finger? Denim feels as good as silk or satin—better! It's more comfortable, and it can be washed in a machine, too," she concluded practically.

"You're introducing a new element into the argument now, to confuse the issue," he objected. "Convenience has nothing to do with it."

"Convenience gives us the real luxury of time. That's the only thing you can't buy."

Tony's fingers formed a steeple, and he regarded her over the top of it. A lambent light shone in his eyes as he prepared to counter her argument. "The *only* thing! Surely all the rest of life isn't for sale! Someone's been leading us astray. I always heard that the best things in life are free. It doesn't cost a penny to look at a sunset or a tree—or even a beautiful woman, as long as you only look. Friendship is not for sale, or true love." He waited expectantly for her reply.

"That's true." Jerri conceded. "And health, too, can't be bought. Those are what I consider the good things in life."

"Let's drink to time and health, to friendship and love," Tony said, lifting his glass to gaze at her.

She looked into the black pools of his eyes, feeling as if she were sinking in over her head. "I'll drink to that," she said, but in a small voice.

The electronic voice suddenly blared forth. "Number seventeen. Number seventeen."

"That's us! Aren't they fast here?" Jerri asked, smiling and revealing the little gap between her teeth.

"Too fast! I would have preferred the luxury of a little longer talk before our summons."

This time Tony reached for the ticket on the table and went to get their pizza. When he returned, he was looking skeptically at the food. "This looks very . . . interesting," he said doubtfully, and set it down.

Jerri thought it must be the excess of anchovies that caused his lack of enthusiasm, for other than that, the pizza looked delicious. The cheese was still bubbling, and the most enticing aroma of spices arose from it. "You forgot to get our plates and cutlery," she said, and with a tsk for his carelessness, she went to get them herself.

She served the pizza, dexterously twining the strings of hot mozzarella around the tip of the serving ladle with the accomplished air of long experience.

She waited with ill-concealed amusement to see Tony's reaction to the highly-seasoned food, but was disappointed. He ate it with relish, and when he had finished the first bite, said only, "Not bad. They're usually so bland. But I don't care for quite so many anchovies."

"They're the best part," she insisted, though she didn't really like a double order either, and had only asked for them to teach him a lesson.

"No, the company is the best part, in my opinion at

least," he countered. He directed a questioning look at her, hinting for agreement that he, too, was congenial.

"It's a change to have someone to talk to. I usually eat alone when I can," she replied ruthlessly.

He sighed and shook his head. "I expect you read or study while you eat. A mere mortal can't hope to compete with the ancient Chinese philosophers in wisdom, of course, but surely there's something to be said for the fact that I'm here in the flesh, and not just words in a book."

She looked up and smiled impishly. "That's true. Lao-tse never reached for the bill."

She noticed that he was staring at her mouth, and immediately closed her lips to hide the bothersome gap between her teeth. She didn't observe that his expression as he looked was one of delight. His next question took her by surprise. "How old are you, Jerri?"

"Nearly twenty-three. Why do you ask?"

"You look younger when you smile," is all he said, but she knew why he said it.

"I know," she answered curtly, almost angrily, and cut a piece from her pizza. She had been hoping he hadn't noticed the gap in her smile, but of course he had. She resented that gap fiercely. "I could have it fixed if I wanted to," she told him. "Mom offered, but . . ."

"Fixed?" he asked, puzzled. "Your smile is perfect the way it is."

"I'm referring to the enormous gap between my front teeth, as you very well know," she said severely. Her jaw stiffened in defiance. "It's a part of me. I decided to live with it."

"A millimeter of space can hardly be called enormous.

It's not the Delaware Water Gap, after all. You can hardly see it," he assured her.

"You saw it well enough!" she pointed out. "You knew what I meant when I said I could get it fixed. Your *smile* is perfect, you said."

"That was the first time I even noticed it, and I'm sure you must have smiled once or twice before now. It's that special, unique touch that sets a woman apart. I wouldn't even think of having it changed if I were you. I hope you noticed I said *changed*, not fixed. Do you feel it makes a difference in your work?" he asked.

"My work?" she asked, frowning. "No, why should it?"

Tony's questioning glance mirrored hers, also turning to a frown of curiosity. "I was referring to modeling."

"Oh, that!" she said, becoming flustered. "No, I'm not really serious about modeling."

"I wondered why a model would have to study so strenuously," he encouraged, obviously expecting to hear her real career plans.

"I guess they wouldn't," she said. "Have another slice of this pizza before it gets cold," she offered, changing the subject.

"Thank you," he said when she served him, "but I don't want the trail of this mystery to grow cold either. What do you plan to do that entails studying every night? Become a philosopher? There doesn't seem to be much demand for them nowadays. I doubt if you'll even get a job, after all your work."

She looked at him uncertainly, trying to decide whether to tell him her real job. There was really no reason not to. He was just a visitor in town, why should he care what she did with her life? But somehow she had the idea he *did* care, and an even stronger premonition that, like Dorothy, he'd disapprove. But she was used to battling opposition.

Jerri lifted her chin, looked him coolly in the eye and said, "I'm a private investigator. I managed to get my license, with my dad's help, but I still have a lot to learn. That's what I'm studying at night."

Tony looked at her for a moment, nodding his head. His expression was enigmatic, not disapproving, not even surprised. "That's interesting," he said calmly. "An unusual choice for a young woman, but then you're obviously an unusual person. I can't say I'm surprised, especially since I thought you'd make a good police officer. But why do you waste your time driving a cab if you already have your license?"

"It helps make ends meet financially when I'm not busy," she admitted. "There's not a great demand for a private investigator in Leamington."

"You should move to a larger city," he said reasonably.

"No!" she exclaimed quickly. "No, I like it here. It's—home, sort of. I used to spend some summers here with my aunt when I was young, and when I finished school I moved here to be with my dad. He's dead now, but I've settled in here. I'm tired of moving all over the place. You just get your clothes unpacked and a little nest prepared and it's time to move on. I've met people here; I have friends. I don't really spend every night with a book."

"What sort of work do you find in Leamington?" he asked.

"Not the violent crimes you'd find in a big city. I'm not really interested in that. I help parents find runaway kids, do the odd jobs for insurance companies, and some security for commercial outfits. That's what I'm studying at night—electronics for alarm systems.''

"But there are companies that do nothing else," he pointed out. "How do people know you're in that business as well?"

"Word gets around in a small city like this," she answered vaguely. "It's the wave of the future."

"From a practical point of view, it would make more sense to forget the sleuthing and concentrate on electronic security," he said.

"Oh, no! I hate electronics!" she said. "It's an unfortunate necessity, but it's the personal contact that I like in my work. It's rewarding to help people."

Tony looked unconvinced, but he didn't argue further. "Do you do anything in the line of industrial espionage?" he asked, and picked up his beer, peering at her over the rim.

"I haven't so far, but I would. I'd take on just about anything except divorce cases, though they pay well," she added sadly.

"You're violently opposed to divorce, I take it?"

"No, it's not the principle of the thing, it's the messiness of it. Proving adultery and things like that can become rather degrading."

"Are you a good private investigator?" he asked.

"I'm still learning, but I'm pretty good," she said. "You have to train yourself to be observant of seemingly insignificant details. For instance, could you tell me who's sitting behind you? Could you describe the people?" she asked, her eyes bright with enthusiasm.

"I can't even see them," he pointed out.

"You saw them when you came in. I noticed your

looking at them, but you didn't really *see*. You didn't observe what they wore, or what they looked like. You couldn't describe them if anyone asked you to,'' she pointed out, with an air of superiority.

"Now don't be too sure about that!" he cautioned. "I'm no slouch when it comes to observing. If I'm not mistaken, the curvaceous blonde in a pink sweater and black slacks rattled the chair behind our table. Am I right?"

"Yes," she conceded, disappointed. "But could you describe the man with her?"

"Was she with someone? I confess I didn't notice, but I could report that her slacks were tight, and either leather or vinyl.''

"And if the man with her was a murderer, you couldn't tell the police whether he was a bald midget or a hairy giant," she said, unhappy with his close scrutiny of the woman.

"I'm sure I would have noticed if he had been that unusual in appearance.''

"He *was* unusual. He has on a big black cowboy hat and a leather fringed vest. You only noticed the blonde because . . . Well, you know what I mean," she said, mocking him with her eyes.

"You're right, I should have at least noticed that she *was* with a man. I wonder what distracted me?'' he asked, smiling intimately in his lazy way.

"Probably the brunette with the bedroom eyes who's serving the pizza," she riposted, since his eyes had slid to the bar a few times as well.

"Verna, you mean?"

"How did you know her name?"

"She's wearing a name tag on her blouse. Don't tell me

you didn't *observe* it when you gave her our order?'' he asked, widening his eyes in feigned astonishment.

''No, I didn't happen to observe her—er, blouse. I was looking at her face. She has a mole on her left cheek. Identifying marks are much more significant than names. You can't change birth marks,'' she added, to bolster her sagging confidence.

''I don't see why a guilty person couldn't stick on a fake mole to distract attention, but I'll grant you that a name can be changed. You've had longer than a few minutes to observe me, Jerri. How would you describe me, if you learned I were—say, an ax murderer? No, don't look at me. Close your eyes and describe,'' he ordered.

She closed her eyes, and had no difficulty at all in visualizing the man across from her. Her instinct was to begin with those molten eyes, but she desisted. ''Male, Caucasian, six feet two, swarthy complexion, dark eyes, about one hundred and eighty pounds, thirty years old.''

''Six feet one inch, one hundred and seventy-five pounds, twenty-nine years old. Not bad!''

''I'm not finished yet. Good teeth, probably capped. No visible birth marks, very natty dresser,'' she added.

''The teeth are my own! And when you throw in that natty dresser bit on top of my swarthy complexion, you make me sound like an escapee from a gangster movie,'' he objected.

''And that's only the physical description,'' she said, opening her eyes to observe him. ''I could throw in that he's very secretive about his business. Probably a gambler,'' she added daringly, and looked for his reaction.

''I should be happy you didn't call me a murderer, I

suppose," he said, smiling. "We're all gamblers of one sort or another."

"*Very* secretive about his business," she said, and scowled at him.

"I'm flattered at your interest. I hope it won't wane when I assure you I'm a legitimate businessman."

"Gambling is legal in some states. I wasn't calling you a crook."

"I'm not a professional gambler, nor even an amateur in the sense we're discussing. Occasionally I take a chance on some business venture. My largest business concern is a steel mill. Lately I've begun branching out into operations that employ my own product. Sorry to disappoint you, Geraldine," he said, leaning across the table and patting her hand.

"I'm not disappointed. Just surprised that you finally divulged your business. Why did you make it such a mystery?"

"I hope to keep it quiet that I'm in Leamington. Now that I know you, and don't want you to labor under the delusion that I'm on half a dozen Wanted-Dead-or-Alive posters in post offices, I thought it time to tell you. But I would appreciate it if you wouldn't tell anyone. It's a deep, dark secret. Mum's the word," he said, putting a finger to his lips.

"Has it got something to do with Mayhew?" she asked.

"Yes, it has."

"Why is it a secret?"

"Because I don't want anyone to know. That's the whole idea of a secret. Rumors can do a lot of damage when delicate negotiations are being prepared."

"I see," she said.

"Now enough about me. Back to the much more important matter of food. Would you care for a spumoni?"

"I'd love it." She smiled. "Do you want me to get it?"

"No, no, I'll get it. I'm trying to create the illusion that we're friends, out on a date. Unlike that cheapskate of a Lao," he added prosaically. "A double scoop for you, I presume?"

"Yes, I don't think I could handle three scoops today," she answered calmly.

Tony soon returned with two double dishes of spumoni, and the subject of their respective jobs was abandoned. Jerri was still curious about what his exact interest in Mayhew might be, but she'd decided he wasn't a crook. In fact, he was nice. She would like him for a friend, and was sorry he'd be leaving soon.

"You still haven't given me any idea how long you'll be in town, Tony," she mentioned after they'd finished the spumoni.

"Long enough to introduce you into the esoteric ritual of proper dining. How about tonight?"

"I'd love to. Oh, I forgot. I'm busy tonight."

"So am I, now that you mention it. How about tomorrow evening?" he asked.

"Are you sure you'll still be here?"

A charming smile started in his eyes, and then slowly developed across his lips. When he spoke, he used that dangerously purring voice that sent shivers down her spine. "Wild horses couldn't drag me away, if you say you'll let me see you tomorrow night."

Jerri felt a little shaken by his expression, but she

answered offhandedly, "What the heck, I can study any time. I accept."

"Good," he said, smiling with satisfaction. "You've saved a team of wild horses a lot of exertion. Where can I pick you up?"

"Since you don't have a car, I'll meet you at the Everett," she suggested.

"Good, can you come at seven? We'll have a few cocktails first, since you *are* old enough to drink. I was a little worried at first that I might be contributing to the delinquency of a minor."

"It's the teeth! I know I should have had them fixed," she complained.

"Not at all. Only think how happy you'll be to have them subtracting years from your age when you hit the dread thirty-year mark," he pointed out.

But thirty was in the dim, distant future, and for the immediate term, Jerri wasn't at all happy to look like an adolescent. She'd wear something very sophisticated and slinky tomorrow night, to show him she wasn't an unpolished juvenile who would be impressed by fine dining. Yech, she hoped he wouldn't want to order Châteaubriand. And there'd be wine that she'd have to pretend to like. She'd had her fill of fine dining in Europe.

It was too late to drive down to the river when they finished lunch, so Jerri took Tony to his hotel and returned the cab to McCane's yard. She felt a little uncomfortable about the large tip Tony had given her, but as he pointed out, he'd been her only customer, and she'd have made as much from several shorter drives.

She received a call from a prospective client when she

returned to her office. A Mrs. Page wanted her to find her lost dog. Jerri suggested the dog pound, but Mrs. Page had already tried there. She insisted the dog had been dognapped, taken from his leash in the backyard. The hook had been undone, not broken by the dog. When Jerri went over to discuss it, she learned that Lothario was only a mongrel, so it seemed entirely unlikely he'd been dognapped with a thought to ransom or breeding. But as the woman was so upset, Jerri agreed to try to help her, and spent the afternoon questioning neighbors and phoning dog pounds in adjacent towns and villages, without making any headway in her first solo case.

Chapter Four

Jerri thought Tony Lupino might be at Elsa Mayhew's dinner party that evening, as he was interested in her factory. It even occurred to her that he might be the guest of honor. She made careful preparations for the party, choosing an elegant misty green gown she'd bought in Italy. All her preparations were in vain. He wasn't there, but she listened to the conversation with interest when Elsa's business troubles were discussed. Not everyone was as considerate as Dorothy in avoiding that troublesome subject.

"When will you be hiring back all the workers you had to lay off, Elsa?" a guest asked her. It was Tom Harrow, a banking friend of Elsa's late husband.

"It begins to look like the twelfth of never," Elsa lamented.

Mrs. Mayhew looked attractive that night. She, too, had taken pains with her appearance. Her coppery hair gleamed like a crown, giving her a regal air as she sat in state at the head of her table. As Jerri looked at her, she realized that Elsa was quite a bit younger than her aunt Dorothy.

"But the strike is over," Tom persisted. "You must be able to meet your commitments now. Is there something else wrong?"

"There's always something wrong," Elsa said wearily. "Now we've got a flaw in one of the motors. We've received a dozen of them back, and we've probably lost those customers. Mr. Wainwright, my chief engineer, says we shouldn't ship any more of those motors till he's got the bugs out, but there's a penalty clause in the contracts, and that means big trouble, so we're still shipping."

"Is it a new motor?" Tom asked.

"No, that's the strange thing. It's one we've been making for four years, and never had any complaints before. Oh, I wish Bill Dallyn hadn't retired when he did! Everything went as smooth as silk when Bill was there. He still had three years to go before his retirement, but after his heart attack, he decided to quit right away. One can hardly blame him," she added forgivingly.

Jerri listened as carefully as she could, especially when the name of Bill Dallyn came up. She was still listening and thinking when Tom Harrow said, "The best thing might be for you to sell the place while it's still worth something."

"I'm sure the plant isn't worth what it was three years ago," Elsa replied. "But if things go on like this, it won't be worth the land it's standing on. I wouldn't say no to a decent offer, but the kind of offers I've received—forget it."

Jerri, being younger than the others, wasn't expected to take much part in this conversation, which left her free to think. And what she soon considered was that Tony Lupino just possibly might be behind the troubles at Elsa's plant. If the trouble continued, he'd be able to buy it at a bargain-basement price. But why had he been to see Bill Dallyn? Surely the *new* chief engineer, Mr. Wainwright, would be responsible for the troubles, if they were being caused purposely, and not just due to accident or carelessness.

On the other hand, Dallyn's early retirement looked suspicious. Had he arranged some sort of sabotage to occur after he retired, to make it look as though he wasn't responsible? Could such a thing be done? Some tinkering with the blueprints might account for it, or some small adjustment to the machinery within the motors.

Most damning of all was Tony's request that she not say a word to anyone. She certainly didn't want to involve Tony if he were innocent, but on the other hand, she couldn't let Dorothy's friend lose her company to a scoundrel.

When Elsa excused herself after dinner and disappeared upstairs, Jerri ran after her. She caught Elsa just as she was entering her bedroom to freshen her makeup.

"Elsa," she said uncertainly, "I don't want to pry into your affairs. It isn't any of my business, but there's a man in town . . . I don't know how to say it exactly. He could be interested in your company. He went to see Bill Dallyn today."

Elsa turned and stared at her, frowning. "Who is this man? What's his name, and how did you find out about him?" she asked.

"I haven't told Aunt Dorothy, but I sometimes drive a cab for Mike McCane. I drove this man to see Dallyn today, and he mentioned your company. He could be planning to buy it," she suggested doubtfully.

"What does he look like?" Elsa asked quickly, apparently concluding that Jerri didn't know his name.

Jerri described him in some detail. "I haven't the faintest idea who he could be," Elsa said, "but he sounds divine. The offer I had was from a Japanese firm, and your passenger obviously wasn't Japanese."

"No, but I suppose he could be working for them."

"I'll phone Bill Dallyn this very night," Elsa decided.

"Do you think that's wise?" Jerri asked. "Dallyn could be involved in the factory's decline somehow."

"Bill Dallyn?" Elsa asked, and laughed. "He was my husband's best friend. Why he was like a father to Hal, and to me, too. No, I trust Bill implicitly, Jerri. Thanks for the information. And I won't tell your aunt about your driving the taxi, but do you think it's wise, my dear?"

"I don't see any harm in it," Jerri defended.

"It can't be as treacherous as tending your snoop shop at least. Are you working on any interesting cases?"

"No, just a dognapping."

"Oh, did Audrey call you?" Elsa asked, surprised.

"Audrey? No, it was a Mrs. Page. Why, did someone else have a dog stolen?"

"Audrey Beaton had her pooch taken from her back yard. Unhooked from the leash—it wasn't a runaway—and it hasn't turned up at the pound. Isn't it strange?"

Jerri got Mrs. Beaton's address to call her later. For the moment, she felt she'd done what her conscience demanded, though she'd been unhappy to do it. She'd told Elsa everything but Lupino's name, and if Bill was the great friend Elsa thought he was, he could supply that.

It was too late to call Mrs. Beaton when Jerri got home, but she did it the first thing the next morning. By that time, Mrs. Beaton had learned that a neighbor's dog had also been stolen from her yard. The three dogs had all gone awol the same night. Jerri studied the map of Leamington that her father had tacked on his wall, and noticed that all three dognappings had occurred in the same part of town, within four blocks of each other. If three had already come to her attention, there were doubtlessly more she hadn't heard of. It looked like a case of mass dognapping, as occasionally occurred, with the stolen animals destined for illicit laboratory use.

She went to the police station with her suspicion, and asked for their help. "Since they did the east side of town the night before last, they'll probably come back and have a go at the west side soon," Jerri suggested.

"That's exactly what I thought," Lieutenant Croft agreed. He was a young officer who had known Joe Tobin and was acquainted with Jerri. "You seem good at your work, Jerri. Why don't you join the force and become a *real* detective?" he asked.

"I *am* a real detective!" she answered, offended by his remark. "It seems to me this case shouldn't be too hard to crack. A pack of dogs isn't exactly easy to conceal, and they wouldn't have gone too far beyond town since they're still in the process of collecting their victims. Why don't you get the State Police to help you check out the countryside? Those dogs have got to be in a vacant barn or something."

"I'm a real detective, too, Jerri," Croft replied, smiling slyly. "You don't have to tell me how to run my business. You private eyes are all alike."

A little thrill coursed through her veins to hear herself

included in the brotherhood of private eyes, even if it had been intended to be a putdown. Jerri spent some time that day driving through the countryside herself, checking into empty barns and vacant farm houses, but without any luck. At least it distracted her thoughts from Tony Lupino, though his face popped into her head often enough to cause dismay. She half wished she weren't seeing him that night, though the other half of her looked forward to it eagerly.

At four o'clock she returned to her office to check for phone messages. She was happily surprised to find a request to phone Earl Malling, one of her father's associates in New York. If Earl had a case that involved any investigation in the Leamington area, he had Joe do the job for him, to save himself the trip. Jerri hoped that this would prove to be the reason he was calling today, and promptly dialed his number.

"I've got a client, a Mrs. Wilbur Smart," Earl said after greeting her. "Her husband has run off and isn't keeping up with his alimony payments. She thinks he might be staying with his sister in Leamington. Care to check it out for me? It'd save me a trip, and make you a few bucks."

"I'd be very happy to, Earl. What's the sister's name?" she asked, pencil poised.

"Mrs. Bill Williams who lives on Baker Street, my client thinks. I guess you could find her in the phone book. All I want you to do is check the place out and see if a guy that fits Smart's description is there. Just let me know, and I'll handle the rest. I'll have his picture in the mail tonight. He's a short guy, five feet five, balding, paunchy, probably wearing a brown suit. She says he always wears brown."

"It's enough to make you wonder why she wants him back," Jerri said, and laughed.

"She doesn't. She just wants her alimony. How's tricks with you, Jerri? You got anything interesting on?"

"Not very interesting," she admitted.

"Be sure to let me know if there's anything I can do for you."

"There is one thing," Jerri said, and was almost surprised to hear the words coming from her lips.

"Say the word."

"Would you check out a Mr. Anthony Lupino for me? I'm a little curious to find out who he is, and where he's from. Try Dunn and Bradstreet for a start. If he's a legitimate businessman, they'd have him on file," she suggested.

"What do you mean? I already did that for your old man," Earl answered, surprised.

"You did?" she answered, more surprised than he. Then Joe *was* involved with Tony! Immediately she thought of the five thousand dollars, and felt afraid. "Did Joe say why he wanted Lupino checked out?"

"He wanted to know who he was working for. Jeez, I miss Joe. He was a great fellow—always had a good story to tell," Earl said.

"I miss him, too, Earl," she said, and felt again that aching sense of loss, but she knew that Earl didn't like to waste time on phone calls, and hurried back to business. "What did you find out about Lupino?"

"The report must be there in the office. He's a big industrialist—steel. He's pulled some pretty sharp deals, but he doesn't have a record."

"Oh, where's he from?" she asked.

"His head office is here in New York, but he has a steel mill in the Ohio Valley. I sent Joe all the dope. Couldn't find out much about his personal life. He's single, a bit of a playboy,'' Earl said.

An angry sneer took possession of Jerri's face as she heard this. "I see. You're sure Joe was working for him?"

"Well now, you've got me there, Jerri. Joe was a bit tight-lipped about the whole thing, now that you mention it. I couldn't tell you for sure whether he was working for or against him.''

"I'll see if I can find the report. Thanks a lot, Earl."

"Any time. What's going on with this Lupino guy anyway? I wouldn't tangle with him if I were you. He plays rough," Earl warned, his voice deepening in concern.

"I'm not sure what's going on, but I'll be careful."

"You do that. Give me a buzz and let me know about Smart, okay?"

"You'll be hearing from me," she said bravely, but her hands were trembling. She hung up the receiver and nervously rubbed her moist palms together.

"He plays rough" kept echoing through her brain. And she was going out to meet him that very evening. She sat perfectly still, her body tense with concentration. Joe had been working for—or against—Tony Lupino. The five thousand dollars had to come from that job. He must have been working for Tony. Elsa was the only person she could think of who might have hired Joe to work *against* Tony, and Elsa didn't seem to know a thing about him. So what was Joe doing for him? If it were something legal and respectable, why wasn't there any record of it in the files? Why hadn't her father told her? Was it possible Tony had managed to corrupt her father? Joe knew he had a weak heart. Maybe he was so worried about her that he'd taken the job for money, so he'd have something to leave her. Oh, but she'd much rather not have the money at all than have had Joe earn it illegally.

She began a systematic search of the office for Earl's report, but it just wasn't anywhere—not in the files, not in the desk drawers, and, as she already knew, not in Joe's apartment either. Was working for Lupino so dangerous or so incriminating that Joe had destroyed the evidence of his involvement? Finally she confronted the awful possibility she'd been trying to hold at bay. Had her father been instrumental in causing the troubles at the Mayhew plant? Was that why all the evidence was gone? What else would pay such a large sum as five thousand dollars? Had Tony bought her father's honor? She felt a pain in her forearms. Glancing down, she noticed that her hands were clenched into white-knuckled fists.

She'd phone the hotel this very minute and tell Mr. Lupino what she thought of him, and cancel the dinner date while she was at it. But a moment's consideration showed her the folly of this plan. How could she ever find out what Tony was up to if she didn't see him? She'd already discovered that he was in steel, and that he was interested in Mayhew. He hadn't wanted to tell her that at first, but she'd finally got it out of him. She'd play along this evening, and see what else came to light.

If her Dad had worked for Tony, then Tony might suspect she knew all about him. But wouldn't he have said something? No, he'd just wait and see if she made any little slips. Maybe that's why he showed interest in her, because he wanted to discover what she knew. That made entirely too much sense to please her. He wasn't really interested in her at all! What did she care what a crook thought of her? But she knew deep down that some part of her *did* care.

When the crook was a devastatingly handsome man with deep liquid eyes that could smoulder one minute and wink with mischief the next, she cared.

She decided to set herself down and give herself a good talking to. *All right then, you're a logical, sensible woman. What's the wise thing to do? Play dumb, obviously. Go along with the game and keep your eyes and ears open. If he's only trying to find out what you know, he's not interested in you personally, and you have nothing to worry about. And if he is interested in you? What harm can he do in a public dining room?* With that settled, it was time to start the investigation for Earl Malling.

After locating Mrs. Williams's address in the phone book, Jerri drove over to Baker Street and found the house, a little brown brick bungalow. She was parked across the street from it for fifteen minutes, but didn't see anyone answering Mr. Smart's description. She'd wait for his picture in the mail and return tomorrow. Or possibly sneak back tonight and peek in the window under cover of darkness. The sooner she found out, the better. She had to establish her professionalism with her associates, and speed was important.

She drove back to her apartment and walked up to the second floor. It was a three-story building which didn't have the luxury of an elevator. After such a hectic day, Jerri needed a Coke to reestablish normalcy before preparing for her date. She pulled the tab of the can and didn't bother with a glass. She removed her boots and sat on her dainty pink velvet sofa, with her feet on the coffee table. Today she didn't take any notice of the pretty room she sat in. The cool liquid slaked her thirst, and soon she felt the aching tension ease from her shoulders. All day, dognapped dogs, runaway husbands, and missing files had vied for attention in her mind with the prospect of tonight's date. At last, she put everything else from her mind and just thought of Tony. The crease between her brows eased, and a provocative smile lifted the corners of her lips.

She didn't really *know* that Tony was doing anything disreputable. It was entirely possible he was innocent of any wrongdoing whatsoever. How had she convinced herself that Joe would go along with anything crooked? It was an insult to the memory of her father. Joe wouldn't even touch a divorce case, much less something like the Mayhew job. The five thousand probably had nothing to do with Tony. Here she was worrying herself into a tizzy, instead of relaxing and enjoying the prospect of this date. At least it wouldn't be a bore, as the dates arranged for her by Dorothy always were.

When she had finished her drink, Jerri took a long, refreshing shower, enjoying the stinging pelt of the water on her back and shoulders. Afterward, she splashed a light cologne on her arms and neck. She had plenty of time, and luxuriated in her preparations. She even painted her fingernails and toenails with a pearly coral lacquer. No plain Jane tonight, she thought with a smile. She applied her makeup with care, using a light hand, and emphasizing her eyes with kohl pencil and a touch of frosted eye shadow.

She sorted through her wardrobe which held an enviable collection of gowns acquired over the years she'd spent in Europe. They were all a few years old, but they were still lovely. How long had it been since she'd bought a new party dress? Or even had any occasion to wear the ones she

owned? Too long! Life was such a round of social doings
when she was with her mother that she'd acquired a distaste
for parties. But tonight she looked forward to dressing up.

Should she wear the sea-foam gown she'd worn to the
Mayhew's last night? It was her favorite, but tonight she
wanted something more sophisticated—a gown that would
throw Tony Lupino for a loop, though she didn't think he'd
succumb easily. Instinctively her hand went to the black silk
gown with the Paris designer label. She'd only worn it
once, because she found it too sophisticated for Leamington, and too mature to suit her, but that's the effect she
wanted tonight.

She laid it carefully on her bed and put on a black lace bra
and panties, dark nylons, and a pair of black patent sandals
with dangerously high heels. Then she took the dress and
slipped it on. It closed with invisible snaps down the front,
hugging her body, fitting closely until it reached her hips
where it flared out gently. The snaps stopped a foot from the
bottom, revealing a flash of leg when she walked.

She stood in front of the mirror and regarded herself
critically. The dress was sleeveless, which was fine, but the
bodice was cut daringly low. The gentle swell of her breasts
was visible even standing up straight. Was it too risqué?
Would it give Tony ideas? She felt a thrill at the notion.
With an insouciant twitch of her shoulders, she thought,
why not? He wouldn't be able to do much about it in public,
and she had every intention of driving herself home.

The unrelieved black of her dress demanded color. She
had a few suitable pieces of jewelry, but after having
proclaimed to Tony her love of simple things, she chose
instead a white silk rose for ornament. She tried it at the

shoulder, then switched it to the left hip, where the dress folded in front.

This created the desired effect, but her hair curling around her shoulders now looked girlishly incongruous. She brushed it up in a swirl and attached it loosely, high on the back of her head. A few curls escaped below her ears and at the nape of her neck, but she let them fall. She didn't want to look too precise, too carefully arranged.

Jerri hardly recognized the cool, elegant woman who gazed back at her from the mirror. The dark arch of her brows above her wide-set eyes and high cheekbones gave her a somewhat haughty air. Her short, straight nose tipped up slightly at the end to add a youthful touch to her appearance. Everything was just as she wanted, as long as she kept her teeth hidden. She didn't even attempt a smile; she didn't want to shake her confidence in herself. She knew she'd need plenty of it before this night was over.

At ten to seven she drew a black cashmere shawl over her shoulders and went to her car.

Chapter Five

The doorman at the Everett Hotel took Jerri's keys to park her car and opened the front door for her to enter the lobby. The Everett might be the finest hotel in Leamington, but it failed to impress a woman who'd visited the best hotels in Paris, Rome, and London. She barely glanced at the chandeliers, the marble floor, or the antique furnishings in the lobby. As she walked to the front desk, she recognized the night clerk, Rob, a friend of her father's whom she had met a few times. Joe had known all the clerks and hotel detectives, whom he called "dicks." They occasionally helped him on a case, and received a fin for their assistance. Joe had been of the old school, and had employed the passé slang which was familiar to Jerri from her long love affair with Dashiell Hammett and Raymond Chandler.

"Hi, Rob," she said, as she approached the desk. "I'm meeting Mr. Lupino. Is he in?" Always observant, she looked to see where Rob turned. His hand pointed to the hook numbered 204.

"There's no key here. I'll just give his room a buzz."

She looked at her watch and noticed she had arrived five minutes early. Arriving early was not sophisticated. "No, just wait a minute," she said quickly.

Rob, who had been examining her, lifted his brows in approval. "Very classy!" he said. "You and Mr. Lupino must be planning to paint the town red."

"What do you take us for? Communists?" she asked, making it a joke, for she was suddenly embarrassed. She didn't like the way Rob was leering at her.

"There's Mr. Lupino now," Rob said, looking toward the elevators.

Tony was hastening forward, glancing at his watch. He looked up and saw Jerri. For a brief moment his face showed considerable surprise, but by the time he reached her, his expression had settled down to a welcoming smile.

"Not only on time but extremely elegant!" he complimented, but then diluted the praise by adding, "Have you been at a funeral? I see you're all in black."

"I'm anticipating a mournful evening," she retorted pertly.

She noticed that Tony was wearing a casual blazer and gray flannels, with only a silk scarf, rather than a tie, at his throat. Suddenly she felt gauche and too dressed up for the occasion, and continued to answer flippantly to hide her lack of ease.

"I thought the whole point of this evening was for you to introduce me to *haute cuisine*. Surely that calls for *haute couture!* Don't tell me you mean to slough me off with a hamburger!" She drew off her shawl and draped it over her arm. "We *are* staying here at the hotel for dinner, I assume? You mentioned their excellent dining room."

She felt a swell of heat within her as his dark eyes traveled slowly from her face and down her neck, to linger over her shoulders and chest before returning to meet her gaze. "I beg your pardon?" he asked, as though overcome by what he had seen.

"Don't overdo it, Tony," she said sardonically.

"It's a little late for me to say the same to you. I'm overwhelmed. I feel we should be dining at the Ritz, speaking French, and drinking nectar."

"Champagne will do just fine. Shall we go?" She tossed him a saucy smile, but with her lips carefully closed.

"Your table awaits, mademoiselle." He made a low bow, offered his arm, and led her in to the dining room.

Jerri had withstood all her Aunt Dorothy's efforts to get her into this particular dining room. She looked around with some interest now. It was a long, high-ceilinged room that still managed to create an intimate atmosphere. It was the subdued lighting that did it, and the cluster of round tables, each covered in white linen, bearing one fresh rose in a crystal vase, and a candle lamp. The tinkle of glasses and cutlery mingled with the hum of subdued voices, while red-jacketed waiters bustled to and fro, carrying covered platters.

It had been a long time since she'd been in a place like this. A soft smile lifted her lips as she gazed around.

"You'll get used to the quiet and inactivity in no time," Tony said. "If you're looking around for where to take your ticket, you can just relax. Those men in red coats will handle our order for us."

She knew from his smile that he was joking, but he *did* think he was impressing her. His air was that of a man conferring a treat.

"No, actually I was looking for the soft drink machine," she answered sweetly.

The maître d' came up to them immediately. "Good evening Mr. Lupino, madame. Your table is ready," he said with an obsequious bow.

Jerri followed him to a table at the back of the room, well away from the dais that held a piano. A musician was just mounting the stairs to it.

The waiter seated them and presented the drinks menu to Tony who handed it back without reading it. "That won't be necessary, Charles. We know what we want. Champagne, isn't it, Jerri?"

"*Merveilleux*," she agreed, using her heaviest French accent.

"The Mumm's will be fine," Tony said aside to the waiter. After the man had left, he turned back to Jerri. "If you're planning to blow me over by a tirade of French, you can forget it. I only speak menu French."

"That's the best kind," she replied, and was glad she hadn't rattled off more French, as she had intended on doing. That would have been too childish and obvious. Tony required a more subtle strategy.

"What have you been doing with yourself all day?" he asked, settling in comfortably.

She leaned her wrists on the table and smiled. "I've gone to the dogs," she said airily.

"I would have to disagree with that!"

"I mean quite literally. I've spent the better part of the

day trying to bust a poochnapping ring,'' she said, and then proceeded to make an amusing story of her adventure. Tony listened with attention.

When she had finished, he said, ''I bet you never thought your work would be so mundane. Here you've been probably seeking high adventure, chasing felons and felonesses, and you end up becoming dog-catcher.''

She was quick to remove this impression. ''That was only one of my cases today. I'm also working with an associate in New York, tracing a runaway husband.''

''That's more like it. Is he wanted by the law?'' Tony asked, but with still a touch of condescension, as though he were humoring her.

''Of course he is. Not paying alimony is a criminal offense,'' she answered curtly.

The champagne arrived, bringing with it a more festive air to the meeting. Taking a sip, her spirits rose as the bubbles tickled her nose, and the crisp, cool liquid bit her tongue. It was almost as good as Coke.

''How did *you* spend the day?'' she asked. Her tone was conversational, but she kept a sharp ear out for his answer.

''I spent a good part of it at a stockbroker's office, monitoring the tape. Talk about mundane!''

''Is something important going on in the world of finance?'' she asked.

''There's always something important going on there. It's a little like detective work, in a way. You try to figure out by the rise and fall of stocks what evil machinations are afoot in boardrooms and who's buying and selling, for what price, and why.''

''Did you learn anything profitable?''

''Fortunes aren't made and lost in a day. It's a matter of

studying the market over a period of time. Ah, here's Charles with the dinner menu,'' he added, as the waiter approached their table again.

Jerri realized she had learned exactly nothing, and to continue the interrogation would look too suspicious, so they discussed the meal instead.

"Here's your chance to practice your menu French" she said, noticing that the menu was printed in French.

"I see they have Châteaubriand,'' he mentioned.

"I was afraid they would,'' she replied, then ran a practiced eye down the menu, unaware of the sudden look of surprise that had flitted across Tony's face. *"Crevettes,"* she read doubtfully. "They'll probably come with tartar sauce. That should be against the law. *Jeune agneau* is a definite no. Who could eat a sweet little lamb? I'm afraid it's going to be the *homard* for me, Tony. They can't do much to destroy a lobster. And a Caesar salad, I guess. How about you?'' she asked, and looked up.

Surprise and amusement warred on Tony's face. "You certainly know your way around a French menu for a girl who was raised in an English boarding school!'' he exclaimed.

"Girls grow up and leave school,'' she pointed out, swallowing her anger at the childish description. Was he blind? She was wearing a dress that would have done justice to Marlene Dietrich.

"True, but I was laboring under the misapprehension that this particular one graduated from the junk food school of fine cuisine. What has old Lao got to say about this decadence?''

"You know what a cheapskate he is,'' she said, and laughed. It was impossible to remember her gapped teeth twenty-four hours a day, but as Tony gazed at her mouth, with a little smile playing on his lips, she remembered it and closed her lips.

When Charles arrived, Tony gave Jerri's order and chose a steak for himself.

"Where did you gain this great familiarity with French menus?" Tony asked idly after Charles had left. "Not in England, I think?"

"In France mostly," she answered briefly. "I lived there for a while."

"And what was Miss Tobin, private eye, doing in France, if I may be allowed to ask?"

"I told you my mom was Polish."

"Yes, but Polish wives of Irish-American husbands, who for some unexplained reason have their daughters in English schools, don't usually live in France," he pointed out reasonably.

She was reluctant to dredge up the past, but she had a feeling Tony wasn't going to be satisfied with a partial answer. "My parents were divorced shortly after I was born. I lived with my Mom, sort of. She aspired to be a jet-setter."

"That's where you acquired your aversion to lavish desires, is it?" he asked quietly.

"I concluded it wasn't worth the effort. She didn't always succeed, which may account for the aversion. Sometimes she just lived in Europe in plain old apartments —those were the happiest times really. But Mom was ambitious, in her own way. In her day, a woman got ahead by marrying a rich man. She married an Italian man, Count Fragliani, and enjoyed quite a few good years." Jerri looked at her hands, but she was seeing her mother, and a wistful expression was on her face.

"Is she married to him now?" Tony asked.

"Oh, no, they broke up years ago. She received a very good settlement, and has lived on that. But she's getting married again soon, to a Frenchman this time."

Tony listened closely, but if he felt sorry for her, he didn't show it. "An unusual upbringing," he said. "I had a fairly conventional one myself, though my father died when I was quite young."

"Where were you raised, Tony?" she asked, happy to divert the talk from herself.

"In Ohio, but I've lived in New York for some time now."

At least that was true, she thought. It agreed with what Earl had told her on the phone.

"It's a long way from Las Vegas," she mentioned. He gave a curious frown, and she explained her thinking. "That's where you do your gambling, you said."

He gave a lazy smile. "I only said it to make your day. You were trying so hard to find out who I was that I decided to entertain you. I seem to recall some rather pointed remark about Atlantic City. You were posing as a boy; I thought I'd pose as a racketeer. I could see your shoulders tense up when I assumed my gangster's voice. I was just going along with the gag. I didn't really go to the Double Decker at all, Jerri. The clerk at the Everett confirmed my suspicion that it was a dive. I just did a bit of work and went to bed."

"That's not exactly the way I remember our conversation in the cab," she countered. "As I recall, I asked you if you were here to do business with Mayhew. Your head swiveled around as if I'd hit you. That's when you started talking about rackets, Tony.''

"That *did* upset me a little," he admitted. "I've already told you my visit here is in the nature of a secret."

"Was it Mayhew you were watching on the tape at the stockbroker's office all afternoon?" she asked casually, lifting her glass of champagne.

"Mayhew isn't on the board. It's a privately-owned company. I have my own company and a few competitors that I have to keep an eye on. Actually I wasn't at the office all day. I rented a car and drove around the countryside a little."

"I thought you didn't drive!" she exclaimed.

"Where'd you get that idea? I never said I don't drive."

"Why did you pay twenty-five bucks an hour to hire a cab and driver, when you could have rented a car for a lot less?" she asked.

"Because you wouldn't have been my driver in that case, Geraldine," he answered reasonably. "Why did you think?" He wore a soft smile, and his eyes glowed as he gazed across the table.

Something in her responded instinctively to that smile, but the questions were still there, nagging. She bit her bottom lip, and lowered her eyes to her glass. The bubbles rose slowly in wavy lines, as they always do in good champagne.

"Are you planning to buy Mayhew?" she asked. The words came out slowly, reluctantly.

"Maybe. It depends on the price. Why do you ask?"

"They're having some trouble at the plant," she said,

still hesitantly, still not looking at him, and treading carefully, as if stepping over verbal landmines.

His hands came across the table and seized hers. She released her hold on the stem of the glass and looked at him. He wore a calm, confident smile. He didn't look like a crook.

"It's kind of you to tell me, but actually I already knew about it. I had a man looking into it for me. Mayhew always had an excellent reputation, till it lost its chief engineer a few years ago. I don't see how it's possible for a company to nosedive so quickly without outside help. Or maybe *inside* help, if you know what I mean." His fingers held hers tightly, and his eyes gazed at her steadily.

"You think someone there is sabotaging the operation?" she asked.

"I'm pretty sure of it. I talked to Bill Dallyn. He's—"

"I know who he is," she interrupted, anxious to hear more.

"Since I've told you this much, and since I trust your discretion, I might as well explain the rest. I want to buy Mayhew, but only if the trouble can be rectified fairly easily. Hal Mayhew was an acquaintance of mine, and while I never met his wife, I don't like to see her cheated out of what Hal built up. If people knew I was here, they'd have an idea *why* I'm here, and that's why I didn't want you to tell anyone. If someone at the plant is purposely botching things up, he'll cover his tracks. Dallyn doesn't see how a certain engine they manufacture could be faulty if it's being produced as it was when he was there. It never gave *him* any trouble."

"How can you find out?" she asked eagerly.

"I'm going to talk to Mrs. Mayhew and get her to let one of my engineers snoop around. He'll be hired, ostensibly as just another engineer, but actually he's one of my brightest employees. He'll soon know what's going on there. Bill Dallyn's arranging it with Mrs. Mayhew tonight."

Jerri smiled a peaceful, beatific smile. All her doubts were explained away, and she hadn't even had to admit to Tony that she had mistrusted him.

"How did you come to suspect all this?" she asked.

"I follow the news in my own industry very closely. I knew Mayhew was having a lot of trouble—trouble that didn't make any sense to insiders. I knew the Japanese had made a ridiculously low offer for the company. The offer was refused, but it was only the low price that Mrs. Mayhew had objected to. I heard she wouldn't say no to a reasonable offer. So I hired a man to ask around and learn what the local scuttlebutt was. I hired a local man since he'd be in the best position to snoop without raising too much suspicion. He knew a lot of the employees, and talked to them in bars and so on—all very casual and informal. He also approached Bill Dallyn on my behalf." He paused before continuing. "I suppose you have an idea who the local man was?" he asked.

"Yes, I noticed Dad spent a lot of time in bars just before . . . You knew he was dead, I presume?" she asked, willing down the lump that rose up in her throat.

Tony squeezed her fingers. "I'm sorry, Jerri. Yes, I did know. He was recommended to me by an investigating company in New York, and they notified me of his death. He did his job well. You can be proud of him," he said approvingly.

"I'm glad. Do you mind if I ask how much you paid him?"

"Five thousand dollars. He was on the case for quite a while. Why do you ask?"

She nodded her head in satisfaction. "I thought so. I couldn't figure out how he'd got so much money in a lump sum."

"I paid him after he made his report. I asked him not to leave any copies around where someone might get hold of them."

"He didn't. I've searched through all his things, and he didn't have your name written anywhere," she told him.

"He was a pro," Tony said, sadly shaking his head. "I told him not to tell anyone, and I guess he didn't even tell his own daughter. He didn't tell *me* he had a daughter. You could have knocked me over with a feather yesterday when you told me your name was Tobin. I wondered if you were any relation to Joe. You don't look much like him," he said, examining her face closely, "though I only met him once, of course. I even wondered, after I learned who you were, if you'd gone out to the airport on purpose to meet me, but when you didn't introduce yourself, I concluded it was just a coincidence."

"I had no idea who you were. The only thing that disappoints me is that Dad didn't trust me to help him," she said, wounded at this slur on her ability. "It's not as if it were dangerous."

"It could have been, Jerri," he countered. "But I imagine the main reason was just that you couldn't really help. It was a matter of hanging out in bars, drinking with the workers from Mayhew, getting their opinions about what was going on, and putting two and two together."

"I guess he would have told me after it was all over," she consoled herself.

"We managed to meet, you and I, even without his help. Let's drink a toast to Joe."

He lifted his glass; she lifted hers, and they clinked them together. "To Joe," they both said, and drank.

The champagne went down easily. The lump in her throat was dwindling. It was good to hear that Joe had finally had one big case before he died. He must have been delighted with it, but he was a good enough detective that he hadn't betrayed his job. She was grateful to Tony for having given Joe that chance to prove himself. Her happiness shone in her eyes.

When the food arrived, they left the matter of Mayhew and Joe behind, and talked about other things. There was a mood of intimacy, as though the discussion had brought them closer together. Tony's "conventional upbringing" was explained in more detail, and she listened closely. She was very impressed with his success story, rising from a fatherless childhood to become a young man working his way through college, and then taking a job at a steel mill to learn the details of the business. He sold insurance at night to make extra money to buy shares, until finally he became the major shareholder of the small private mill. He emphasized his luck—an uncle had left him some money—but she knew a lot of hard work and effort must have gone into it as well. It seemed almost an inhuman amount of work and risk taking.

"Well, I admitted I'm part gambler," he reminded her. "The mill was losing money when I bought in. Plenty of people thought I was crazy, but I knew it could be turned around, and we did it. Not just myself, I have partners. Some people in the business hinted that my partners and I dealt in an underhanded way, but we offered what we could afford. To tell the truth, we were amazed when our offer was accepted. I've heard the words 'sharp' and even 'ruthless' used to describe me. I console myself that it's sour grapes doing the talking.''

She listened, but didn't reveal to him that she had heard similar remarks from her associate in New York. She, too, now believed that the remarks were sour grapes.

The waiter came to affix a bib around Jerri's neck when her lobster arrived. ''Now that style really suits you,'' Tony joked. ''You look all of five or six years old. Mind you, I regret the loss of your décolletage.''

''Why, thank you, I think. I'm wearing my best bib and tucker on purpose to impress you,'' she answered, unoffended. The champagne had taken the edge off her nervousness, and the air of camaraderie had made her forget all about her teeth.

''Which part is the tucker?'' he asked.

''I was afraid you'd ask. I have no idea,'' she admitted, neatly cracking off a claw from her lobster. ''How's your steak?''

''Dry,'' he replied, even though appetizing pink juices streamed from it. ''What I mean is, we're out of wine. Shall we make it another champagne, to avoid puzzling over what kind and color of wine suits us both? Champagne goes with everything, my knowledgeable friends tell me.''

''Like Coke,'' she added. ''I've had my quota of wine; I think I'd like a Coke.''

He shook his head ruefully. ''Just when I thought you

had a touch of sophistication! I really must take your gastronomic education in hand, young lady,'' he said, with mock severity. He raised his hand and beckoned the waiter.

"Alas, too late," she informed him. "If the vineyards of France couldn't seduce me, do you really think the fleshpots of Leamington will accomplish it?"

He measured her with a glance of friendly calculation. "New York has a better class of fleshpot," he said simply, but she read a suggestion in it that she might, at some future time, see him in New York.

"May I have a Coke, please?" she asked the waiter when he returned.

Tony shook his head in resignation and added, "Make it two. If you can't lick 'em, join 'em. I'll be darned if I'm going to get tipsy while you're stone cold sober."

"You wouldn't want to do that. I might take advantage of you," she riposted.

"I should be so lucky! I've been wondering how to top off this sybaritic evening," he went on, looking at her for a suggestion. "The hotel doesn't have dancing during the week, and you're much too beautiful to expose to the clientele at the Double Decker, if the clerk here at the hotel is to be believed. Do you have any ideas?"

She glanced up from her struggle with the lobster and said, "I'm not really dressed for bowling. Too bad. And the library closes at nine . . ."

He looked at her impish smile, and refused to satisfy her by being outraged at these pastimes. "I imagine there's a pinball alley somewhere in town," he suggested blandly.

"Two of them, but they both have strict dress codes. Did you happen to pack a black leather jacket and jeans in your luggage?"

"I knew I forgot something!"

She looked at him uncertainly, then came to a decision. "If you weren't such an insufferable snob, I'd offer to take you on a case with me," she said.

A flash of interest gleamed in his eyes. "A stake-out for the dread dognappers?" he asked.

"No, actually I planned to do a little window-peeking later tonight. I'm in a bit of a hurry to see if the runaway husband is in town." She looked, waiting to see his reaction to this activity.

"I couldn't let you go alone!" he said at once. "Include me in. Ah, here's our can of wine," he said, as the waiter came back with the Cokes, not actually in cans, but already poured into glasses.

"What vintage is this, Charles?" he asked, sipping it as though testing a rare wine.

"This year's, Mr. Lupino. Coke is like new Beaujolais. It's best drunk fresh. *Bon appetit*." Unperturbed, Charles bowed and left.

"That'll teach me to be a smart aleck." Tony laughed, and quaffed his drink.

After their plates were cleared, they dallied over dessert and coffee, talking about books and movies, places they'd been and places they wanted to go. A languorous mood of contentment and well-being hovered over the table, but beneath it, some excitement was beginning to build. Tony held her hands in his warm fingers, and his eyes seldom left her face. When Charles returned and asked in a haughty tone if they would care for a liqueur, or another soft drink if they preferred, they decided it was time to leave.

"Do you plan to do your window-peeking dressed the

way you are, or do you change into a trench coat and slouch hat for it?'' Tony asked.

''No, that's my uniform for tailing suspects,'' she replied, acknowledging his dig by a lift of her arched brows. ''I'll just slip off my high heels and go as I am.''

His eyes strayed over her face and down to her neckline. ''I'm only on the second floor of the hotel myself. I'd be happy to supply a ladder if you'd like to continue your job after I retire.''

''Would I be likely to see something interesting?'' she asked, turning the joke back on him. ''I didn't think the Everett Hotel had that kind of reputation.''

''It's high time something be done to enliven its reputation,'' he parried. He beckoned the waiter again and settled the bill.

Jerri took out her makeup and repaired her lipstick at the table in the Parisian style, not hurriedly or secretively, but with apparent unconcern for anyone watching her. Tony wore a bemused smile.

''A very pretty performance,'' he congratulated after she rubbed her lips together to distribute the color evenly, ''and highly erotic.''

''Erotic?'' She laughed and snapped her compact closed. ''Hardly. I was just checking out the couple behind us in my mirror. Joe had that woman for a client once, but don't ask why! Discretion is our motto.''

''I'm about to give up on you. Don't you ever think of anything but business?''

''Of course I do, Tony. I'm thinking right this minute that if we hurry, I'll be home in time to watch *The Maltese Falcon*. It's on the late show tonight,'' she added.

A smile lit his face. ''Oh good! It's one of my favorites.''

"We have something in common. We'll both watch it," she said, gazing into his eyes. His fingers tightened on hers, and he leaned slightly forward. His lips opened to make some affectionate comment, but she spoke before he could do so. "You in your room, and I at home in my apartment. I'll think of you," she added softly, and pulled her hands away to arrange her shawl over her shoulders, while he drew a long breath and held it.

"One of these days, Geraldine . . ."

Chapter Six

Jerri sat at the wheel of her father's unobtrusive car, turning onto Baker Street. "It's that house, second from the corner on the left," she told Tony. "You see if there's any sign of life while I drive by slowly."

"It's dark. They must have gone to bed," Tony said after they had cruised past. But he probably had only been paying scanty attention, Jerri thought, unsatisfied with his answer.

"Nobody goes to bed at ten o'clock," she objected. She drove past a few more houses and coasted to a stop. Turning off the lights and rolling down the car window to crane her neck back, she cried, "There! I told you! There's one light burning in the back. That'd be the den. They're probably watching TV. Come on." She turned off the engine and reached for her door. "Don't slam it when you get out," she ordered, wiggling her toes out of her sandals.

Her heart beat quickly, not with fear, for it wasn't a dangerous assignment, but with the excitement of doing her job, of trespassing, and generally behaving in a surreptitious manner. She slunk through the shadows of the night, with Tony beside her. A quick glance up and down the street showed her they were unobserved. When they reached the driveway that ran alongside the house, Tony took her hand, and they fled toward the backyard, where the light had shone in.

Because there was a set of concrete steps that ran down into the yard, Jerri realized that the window was set up higher than she'd initially thought from the car. It was about a foot and a half above eye level, and even Tony couldn't see in.

"It's too high," she whispered. "We'll need something to stand on. Maybe there's a garbage can or something."

It was impossible to see the details of the tree-shaded yard, so they stole softly away from the window, pacing systematically up and down the yard, looking for something to give them height.

"I can lift you up," Tony suggested.

"It looks as if you'll have to. This yard is as clean as a whistle. There's nothing but grass and trees. Let's go."

They went quietly to the window and listened for a moment. There was no sound from within. Tony reached out his arms and encircled Jerri in them. "This is going to be even more fun than I thought," he murmured into her ear.

"What are you doing?" Jerri whispered, pushing him away.

"I'm going to lift you up to peek in the window, remember?" His head was hovering just inches above hers.

The shadows lent an eerie, unreal flavor to the escapade. Even as he spoke, he was pulling her more closely into his arms, and his head began to lower to hers. She felt a weakening of her resolve, a rampant curiosity to experience his kiss, and was angry with herself.

"For heaven's sake, we're working!" she exclaimed brusquely, and pushed him away.

"You're always working, Geraldine. I don't usually advocate mixing business and pleasure, but in this case, I'll make an exception."

She ignored his remark entirely. "Lock your hands together, make a stirrup with them, and I'll put my foot in it. Then you can boost me up and I'll grab at the window ledge," she explained.

"My way would be more fun," he objected, but he did as she asked.

Even doing things her own way, there was some intimacy in the procedure. She had to steady herself by putting her hands on Tony's shoulders, and as she leaned forward, she felt something brush her throat, and move slowly downward. She thought it was his lips, but decided that ignoring it was the proper course. There was one worrisome moment as he lifted his hands while she was perched precariously on them, when she thought she was going to tumble to the ground. She grabbed his head, and accidentally put one finger in his eye. A muffled complaint sounded loud in her ears.

"Shhh!" she cautioned, and steadied herself against the window ledge.

The window was covered with a gauzy curtain that allowed her only an indistinct view of the room beyond.

The only thing she saw clearly was the TV set and a vacant chair beside it. Mr. Smart, if he was there, must be on a chair or sofa right beneath the window. She leaned carefully forward till she felt the cool touch of glass against her forehead. Yes, there were two heads visible on the sofa below. A man's and a woman's.

She stood irresolute. Any slight noise would bring him to the window, and though she wanted to see his face, she didn't want him to see her.

"Can you see anything?" Tony asked in a low voice.

"I think he's there, but I can't see his face," she whispered.

"This isn't very comfortable, Geraldine. Either tap at the window to make him look, or get down," Tony said, his voice sounding somewhat strained.

She stood undecided for a moment, looking around the yard. Her eyes were more accustomed to the darkness now, and shapes were beginning to become clearer. Was that, by any lucky chance, a wheelbarrow in the back corner of the yard, beside the hump that must be a compost pile? She was struck by the haunting quality of the yard, dimly lit by white moonlight. A weeping willow tree lent a truly Gothic air to the place. And as she looked, something small and dark speedily swooped out of the silver-gray sky. It seemed to be heading straight for her. A bat!

Her heart shrank, and it took all her willpower not to shriek out loud. Joe had told her a story, probably untrue, of a woman who got a bat entangled in her hair and had to have it cut out. The thing swooped past, not even touching her, but coming close enough that she reached out to swipe it away from her. She wobbled on her perch, and Tony's hand instinctively grabbed at her calf to steady her. This, of course, caused her perch to disappear, and suddenly she was tumbling down on his head.

She slowed her fall by grabbing at Tony's shoulders, and simultaneously he caught her in his arms. There was a scuffling sound as he balanced his weight to catch her. For one fleeting moment they stared wide-eyed at each other in the dull shaft of filtered light from the window. Her heart was hammering, but the strangest thing of all was that she felt a nearly uncontrollable urge to laugh out loud. She knew from Tony's strained face that he was struck by a similar urge. To contain their laughter, she buried her face in his shoulder, and he pressed his lips tightly against her throat.

Was it only the effort to suppress laughter that caused those lips to move so warmly? When the movement rose in a sure line up toward her lips, she knew the mood had changed.

"Better put me down," she whispered.

Tony made a sweeping circle away from the window. As he moved, Jerri's foot hit the wall. It was unclear which made the louder noise, her howl of protest or the thump of her foot against brick. Tony was releasing her rather abruptly when they heard the unmistakable sound of approaching footsteps from inside the house.

"Run for cover!" he exclaimed, not bothering to lower his voice. He took her hand and they darted back into the concealing shadows of the yard. Jerri's heart was doing aerobics in her chest, and in spite of the excitement, or because of it, a giggle escaped her lips.

Tony's hand closed over her mouth. "Shhhh, Jerri. Do you want to blow it?" he whispered out of the side of his mouth. She clenched her jaw shut to hold in the nervous laughter, and watched the back door of the house. Tony kept his hand over her lips, while his other hand held hers in a tight grip.

A light went on inside the door, then almost immediately, the back porch light went on. The door opened and a man's head came out. He looked all around, then stepped out onto the porch. As he stood in the pool of light from above, Jerri silently checked his description. About five feet five, balding, paunchy, mid-forties. It had to be Mr. Smart! A sense of exhilaration surged up in her.

The short, portly man looked around once more, muttering to himself, then went back in, and the lights were extinguished.

"It's him!" Jerri said, her voice low but triumphant.

"Good. Can we blow this joint now?" Tony asked, his voice unsteady with mirth.

"We'll wait a minute in case he's looking out the window."

Tony's arm stole around her waist, pulling her against him, but she was taut with tension, too excited for romance. They stood quietly for a moment, till Jerri felt sure the coast was clear. Then they went back up the stairs, out of the yard, crept along the driveway, and rushed across the street to the car.

They were in the middle of the road when the front door of the house opened, and the portly man came out. "Hey, what are you kids doing here?" he shouted after them.

Tony headed straight for the car, but Jerri pulled him past it, down the street.

"Are we going to make our getaway on foot?" he asked, surprised.

"Let him think we're a couple of kids. If we get into the car, he might realize he's been found out and take a powder," she answered in a low voice.

"You think of everything. What the devil happened to make you lose your balance at the window?"

"I saw a bat."

"You never cease to amaze me, Jerri. Trespassing and window-peeping you take in stride, yet you're afraid of a bat?"

"I wasn't afraid! Just surprised. Besides, if they get caught in your hair, it's hard to get them out."

"That's an old wives' tale. Bats operate on an advanced form of radar," he scoffed.

When they reached the corner, Jerri turned and slowed down, rather than continuing down the street. "If he's watching, he'll go back in when we disappear," she explained. Once around the corner, she stopped and hid behind a tree to check out the house. Within half a minute, she heard the door close, and she breathed easier.

"Does this mean we can get the car now, I hope?" Tony asked.

"Of course not! He might still be watching from the window. He's not *innocent,* you know. He probably suspects his wife has had him followed. 'Suspicion haunts the guilty mind.' That's the only bit of Shakespeare Joe knows—knew," she corrected herself. There had been something strange, incomplete about this whole escapade, and she realized suddenly what it was. Joe wasn't here to share it. He'd never be here again. The lively presence of Tony had blown it from her mind, but she now knew what had been in the back of her mind, and was saddened.

Tony's fingers curled around hers in understanding. "He'd be proud of your work tonight," he said softly.

"I botched it by being afraid of the bat, but at least I spotted Smart, and can verify it tomorrow when I get his picture from New York. Case closed, as far as I'm concerned," she said with satisfaction.

"You weren't afraid of the bat, just surprised," he reminded her. "Mind you, if your surprise at a bat sends you into such a paroxysm, I dread to think what your shock at encountering a criminal with a gun might do to you."

"It's never happened," she said, but suddenly realized that it was something to consider. Peeking in windows was fine, rather fun, in fact, but other aspects of her chosen career made her wonder a bit about her suitability for it.

"I hope for your sake it never does. Do you carry a gun, Jerri?" he asked. A worried frown crossed his brow.

"Not usually," she admitted, but, in fact, she had never used her gun once. She had taken target practice as part of her training, but she disliked handling guns.

"Shall we go and get the car now?" Tony asked. "Why don't you let me go alone? He saw two of us. It might throw him off if only one shows up to retrieve the car."

"Okay, but take your jacket off. The white shirt will add to the confusion," she pointed out and gave him the keys.

"I'll be back in a minute." He removed his jacket and handed it to her.

While she stood alone waiting, she kept thinking about guns. Joe was always talking about the big case, the one that would establish a reputation, but a big case would involve guns. Would she have the nerve to use one if necessary? She certainly didn't want to go on forever with this hand-to-mouth existence she lived, but something in her drew away from the sort of high adventure that required guns.

She was relieved when her car nosed around the corner to distract her from these troublesome thoughts. She hopped in and they drove off.

"Is it home, Jerri, or do you have any more business to do tonight?" Tony asked.

"I'd like to take a drive around the west end of town, the residential part, if you're not in a hurry," she answered doubtfully. She wasn't sure Tony was enjoying the evening as much as she was.

"What are we looking for? A van or paneled truck, I assume, since it's the dognappers we're after."

"I'll be happy to drive you back to the hotel if you're tired of this, Tony," she suggested. "This may not be your idea of a thrilling evening."

"Not at all! Playing cops and robbers is infinitely preferable to sitting alone in an hotel room. You don't think I plan to miss the thrill of the chase, do you? This could be much more exciting than playing Peeping Tom. With luck, we may end up being chased by a pack of mad dogs. But next time give me some advance warning and I'll dress for it," he said.

"Don't worry about being chased. If I see anything suspicious, I'll call in the cops. They're supposed to be patrolling the area tonight," she added matter-of-factly. "Hang a left here, Tony."

"Do I make a good getaway man?" he asked, smiling softly in the darkness.

"Super. I couldn't do better myself."

"High praise indeed, bungler! After we make a citizen's

arrest of the dognappers, I plan to toast the evening's work with a Coke. That seems to be the 'in' drink with private eyes this year.''

"If we catch them, the drinks are on me," she offered, laying her head against the seat to relax. She realized her hairdo had become unhinged, and removed the last few pins, letting her hair stream around her shoulders.

They drove up and down the designated area for fifteen minutes without seeing any suspicious van, but they did encounter the police.

"That's two cruisers they've got out. I don't think they really need our help," Tony mentioned.

"That's not two cruisers. It's the same one we saw before. Didn't you notice the license number?" she asked, pretending to be astonished at his lack of observation.

"If I ever need an investigator again, I know who I'll hire," Tony said, conceding her triumph.

"You *do* need one," she pointed out.

He turned to her, a surprised question on his face. "I do? Tell me about it."

"You could use an inside man at Mayhew."

"I've already hired one, remember?"

"He's an engineer. A professional would notice more details. I could pose as a secretary. I type," she added, peering to see his reaction to her suggestion.

"Here I thought you were just another pretty face!"

"I could see right away no one would ever make that mistake about you!" she riposted swiftly.

"I hope not! Are you hinting you find me less than attractive?" he asked, turning to her with a wry expression.

"Not really. I'm hinting that I don't like to be called a pretty face. I hope there's more to me than that."

"I hope so, too. A pretty face unattached to a body is no good to man or beast. At ease, Geraldine," he added, reaching to grab her fingers. "I see you're preparing to launch an attack on my chauvinism. I was kidding. When a man knows a woman has nothing to offer but her beauty, he makes sure not to mention the fact."

"We seem to have run into a diversion here," she said, to return to business. "We were talking about your needing a private investigator."

"No, we were talking about my already having one. We can't plant too many new people inside or someone will begin to wonder. Mayhew isn't doing much hiring these days. Laying off is more like it," he pointed out.

"No one would ever suspect a secretary," she persisted. "There are times when men's erroneous opinions about women's intelligence can be put to advantage."

"Thanks, but I really don't see how you could help," he replied firmly.

"Secretaries have access to files . . ." She let it hang suggestively.

"The man I'm looking for wouldn't be dumb enough to file his crimes under C."

"No, he'd be more likely to hide the evidence in his desk, which I could very easily open at lunch hour, or after five," she parried.

"Let me think about it. I'll let you know, okay?" He turned a bland smile on her, which she interpreted as a pretense to put her off. And if he'd been able to see her face, he would have realized that she had no intention of abiding by his decision.

As he was trying to find his way out of the residential section of town, failing to observe the stubborn set of her chin, she had to give him a verbal hint of her feelings. "Does that mean don't call you, you'll call me?" she asked bluntly.

"You'll certainly be hearing from me," he answered ambiguously.

This caused the conversation to flag. When Tony reached Main Street, Jerri said, "I'll drop you at the hotel. It's just another block." Her tone was slightly annoyed.

"What, no Coke? We had partial success," he reminded her.

"I'm not fit to be seen in public. My hairdo's shot and my feet are dirty. My stockings are full of runs, too."

"I'd be surprised if they'd let us into the pinball alley, the way we look right about now," he joked, trying to rally her back into humor. She remained mulishly silent, and he forged on. "But come to think of it, our appearance wouldn't stand in the way of having a Coke at your place, while we watch *The Maltese Falcon*. And don't try to palm me off by saying you don't have any. I bet you have Coke for breakfast."

"Never, it doesn't go with cereal. I tried it."

"We could pick up a carton," was his last effort.

Jerri felt a burning desire to help finish the case Joe had begun for Tony, and she also felt that if she had him alone for half an hour, she could persuade him to let her do it. He was obviously surprised when she relented. "I guess we've earned a nightcap," she said.

She directed him to her apartment and led the way upstairs. Her rooms were small, but that was the only thing modest about them. When she had decided to make her permanent home here in Leamington, in this set of rooms, she had taken the trouble to make them attractive. Her Aunt

Dorothy had been helpful in supplying her overflow of furnishings, and she'd directed her to secondhand and antique stores to fill in the spaces. A small loveseat of Dorothy's had been recovered in rose-colored velvet; a dainty French provincial coffee table was placed in front of it. The table held a collection of pretty porcelain figurines Jerri had acquired over the years in various countries. Although it wasn't a Persian or anything grand, her carpet was a good white shag that blended with the feminine surroundings. A few attractive reproductions in antique frames decorated the walls, and a highboy bought at an auction in Leamington held more of her porcelain collection. At night, in the soft glow of subdued lamplight, the apartment looked elegant.

She noticed Tony looking around, and wondered what he thought of it, but he didn't give his opinion. "Just make yourself at home and I'll get the can of champagne," she said, dropping her shoes at the door. "But first, I'm going to slip into something comfortable."

She went to tidy herself before rejoining him. She removed the fancy black dress, and slipped on a navy jersey, blue jeans, and moccasins and went to the kitchen for the drinks, thinking of ways to persuade Tony to hire her. When she returned, Tony was fingering a blue delft potpourri pot that decorated the sofa table.

"Lovely," he said, looking up. His gaze encircled the room, stopping at a painting here, a bookshelf along the far wall, a brocade chair in front of the window. "It's not the setting I pictured you in, somehow. It doesn't go with your style." His gaze returned to her, and his lips parted in a half smile as he noticed her change of clothing. "Of course you actually have two very distinct styles. It was the present one

I was referring to, Geraldine. When a lady says she's going to slip into something comfortable, she doesn't usually refer to jeans.''

"True, she usually means the most uncomfortable peignoir she owns, but I don't happen to possess a peignoir. And I doubt if I'd be comfortable in it if I did." She handed him the drink and sat beside him on the sofa.

"How am I supposed to understand you if you go around saying what you mean?" he asked. "That's putting your guest at an unfair disadvantage." As he spoke, he moved along the sofa and slid an arm around her.

"You'll catch on to my idiosyncracies in no time," she replied, removing his hand. "When I agreed to give you a drink, Anthony, I meant a drink, period."

"*Anthony?*" He removed his arm and returned to his former position a few inches away from her on the sofa.

"The Anthony was to repay you for Geraldine. Nobody calls me that."

"It appeals to the Irish part of me. I didn't mean to raise your hackles. Let's drink to a better mutual understanding between us." He lifted his glass in a toast before drinking.

"I'll drink to that," she said, and followed his example.

Silence settled around them. This wasn't helping her cause at all, so she arose to put on some music. In Europe she'd fallen under the spell of Ravel, and "La Valse" was on the turntable. As the heady strains of the full orchestra swept into the room, she returned to the sofa.

"You continue to surprise me at every turn," Tony said. He wore a curious smile, tinged with admiration. "I thought I was the only person who loved this piece."

"It's magic," she said simply.

"I agree. I'll be quiet and let us both enjoy it."

It had been a long day. Jerri closed her eyes and rested her head against the back of the sofa. But it was impossible to remain passive while that wonderful music surged and rose and swelled, creating an achingly nostalgic billow around her. The music evoked, in her mind's eye, the lovely ladies of *fin-de-siècle* Austria in their crinolined skirts, circling in the arms of their cavaliers. Count Fragliani had explained it all to her. He'd been a great lover of classical music.

When she felt Tony's hand on hers, she knew that he, too, was infected by the music, she silently rose to waltz with him. It was simply impossible to sit still. He held her lightly in his arms, with two inches of space between them, as the old code decreed. Together they wheeled and whirled the length of the room, turning dexterously to avoid collision with the furniture, while the music rose irresistibly to a feverish crescendo.

''Now comes the sad part,'' she whispered.

After things reached a zenith, they had to descend again, and it was all there in the music. Strange minor keys surfaced, haunting, eerie, and vaguely menacing. The tempo became uncertain till the music became a drunken whirl. It sounded like organized chaos, and always reminded Jerri of her mother, reeling from city to city, chasing the elusive shadow of happiness. Simple contentment was never enough for Marie. She wanted it all, and she'd probably end up with nothing.

They waltzed with the music, swirling in dizzying circles till Jerri felt like a puppet gone out of control, her head spinning, and her breath catching in her throat. It was only Tony's arms that kept her from falling. When the music stopped, he pulled her against him and her head rested on his shoulder. She felt his hand in her hair, winding it around his fingers, but was too breathless to speak. Who would there be to catch her mother when the music stopped? She shouldn't have played this piece, at least not when Tony was here. She swallowed down the lump in her throat and finally lifted her head from his shoulder.

As she did, his palm cupped the back of her head, and held it steady while his lips descended to hers. It eased the aching loneliness, to have a warm human being with her at this moment. She accepted his kiss, savored the comfort of his arms, and held him tightly against her to ward off the sadness of being alone. And Joe was gone now, too. Oh, darn it, I won't cry. Not now! His lips moved on hers, and his arms strained against her, fitting her body to the contours of his. She immediately forgot the loneliness. His touch was like the magic of Ravel's music, and just as intoxicating.

A tumultuous excitement grew in her, encouraged by his hand's pressure on her back. His lips hardened in demand now, his tongue flickered gently, insistently at her lips, till she could no longer hold out against him. He possessed her mouth, filled it with insinuating motions that awakened her to the danger of this virile consolation she'd accepted. When she tried to withdraw, his arms tightened even more, and she gave in to the pleasure of his embrace.

It felt wonderful, the firm, warm steadiness of his body against hers. But there were also his lips that incited her to madness, his hands that were finding their way under her jersey, caressing the velvet softness of her back with light strokes, then trailing down the sides of her body, swooping in at her waist with a crushing strength. She wasn't used to such passionate consolation, or the dangerous ideas that fired within her. With her resolve dwindling, she put her hands on his and pulled them away, but he hung on to one hand and led her to the sofa.

"Shall we have a drink to keep us sober?" he asked, his dark eyes glowing, observing her with unblinking steadiness, till she felt shy under his scrutiny. She didn't answer, and neither of them reached for their glass. "Or shall we continue to intoxicate ourselves?" he asked softly, pulling her back into his arms.

She had every intention of resisting, but her body refused to obey her commands. Her willful arms went around his neck. She wanted to run her fingers through his thick, black hair, had been wanting to ever since she'd met him. Its rough texture surprised her, but perhaps the gentleness of his embrace surprised her even more. A light patter of kisses rained on her eyes, the tip of her nose, the corners of her lips, while he spoke soft words of endearment. And all the while she felt he was holding himself in check, tailoring his moves to her mood.

When he lifted his head and questioned her with those dark, seductive eyes, she took his chin in her fingers and shook it playfully. She had to break this mood of enchantment.

"Drink your Coke, Anthony. It's time for you to go."

"If you insist on saying what you mean, the least you could do is say something nice."

"I had a wonderful evening. Is that nice enough for you?"

"No, let's make it an unforgettable evening," he bargained, and swept her back into his arms, all tenderness abandoned now. His lips scorched hers, and with one arm holding her securely, the other slid under her jersey. She quivered as his fingers moved in a stroking, rhythmic motion across her back, creeping slowly, with inexorable sureness to her breast. A charge of electrical force shot through her. When his thumb brushed her tense nipple, she was sure he could sense the response that rippled through her. It was an agonizing ecstasy so pronounced it almost hurt.

Her lips opened, as though giving permission for these passionate intimacies. Around them the swells of violins and cellos reverberated and hung tantalizing on the air, encouraging them to rapture.

When Tony lowered her against the back of the sofa, the luxuriously soft pillow of velvet brushed her cheek, to add to the enchantment. The lamplight shone from behind Tony, creating a halo around his head, and casting his face into shadows, so she couldn't recognize his features. It was like making love with a complete stranger. For a moment he sat as still as a statue, looking at her, then his head lowered to hers, and the excitement drove through her.

But she was uneasy now. That unsettling instant of not seeing him, not recognizing him, sent off warning bells. She didn't really know him. He was hardly more than a stranger—how could she abandon herself to him? As he began to reach for her, she put her hands against his shoulders and pushed him back with enough force that he gave way.

He looked at her intensely for a moment, then said, "Okay, I can take a hint when I'm clobbered over the head with it."

He sat back, away from her, and she rose to a sitting position, more embarrassed than he was, judging from his calm expression.

"Since the fun and games are over, aren't you going to put your proposition to me now?" Tony asked blandly. Her mind had strayed so far from business that it took a moment to understand him. "That *is* why you suddenly relented and let me come up here, isn't it?" he asked, his expression unreadable.

"What are you talking about?" she parried, but her guilty eyes betrayed her.

"About your wanting to go to Mayhew to spy around. Now that I know how resourceful you are, I'm convinced you'll end up there, with or without my help, so . . ."

"So you agree?" she asked hopefully.

"You might as well know what you're looking for."

"Engineering prints, blueprints, specifications—something like that?" she prodded.

"Engineering secretaries are specially trained. There's a technical side to their work, so that an untrained secretary wouldn't be hired in that department. They do have a secretarial pool, though, where you could be slipped in. That way, you'll be working in various parts of the company. If you keep your ears open, you might pick up something of use."

"When can I start?" she asked eagerly.

"I'll have to arrange it with Mrs. Mayhew, who'll have to arrange it with personnel. Give me a day or two. I'll be in touch."

Tony stood up to take his leave, and Jerri rose to go with him to the door. "Thanks again. I had a wonderful time," she said.

He wore an enigmatic smile. "We'll do it again very soon. I'll phone you tomorrow. Sleep tight, Geraldine."

He placed a kiss on his finger and transferred it to her

lips. It was a strange way to kiss her good-bye. Strange and oddly touching. She felt a funny ache after he'd left, until she remembered she'd accomplished her aim in asking him up here. But that realization didn't cheer her as it should have. Her aim had shifted. Working for him wasn't the goal now. She wanted more from him than that—a lot more. And she wanted to give him something in return, too, but she dared not ask herself what.

Her feelings were so confused that she didn't even remember to watch *The Maltese Falcon* which she'd been waiting three days to see. The fact that Tony had guessed her reason for inviting him upset her. But when she realized she had her chance now to prove herself as a detective, a small smile peeped out.

Chapter Seven

Jerri enjoyed two successes the next day at work. When the photograph of Mr. Smart arrived from New York, it verified that the man she had seen the night before was indeed the man Earl Malling was looking for. She phoned Earl who was impressed with her performance.

"Good work, Jerri," he congratulated. "If you ever decide to come to the big city to work, look me up and I'll see what I can do for you. I could use a sharp gal like you."

"That's nice to hear. I'll keep it in mind," she answered, smiling from ear to ear.

The other success involved the ring of dognappers, who'd been caught the night before. Lt. Croft from the Police Department called her.

"I'm surprised you caught them, after you lit up the whole neighborhood with a marked patrol car," she mentioned. "How come you didn't send in an unmarked car? That red light should have been enough to scare them off."

"The patrol car wasn't after the dognappers. There were some kids in the neighborhood making mischief, and the car was after them. We caught the dognappers this morning around four. I take it you were out looking yourself?"

"It's my case, too. Was Mrs. Page's dog with the pack?

"Come down to the pound and have a look. We've got eighteen mutts here howling their heads off. Anyway, I just called to thank you, Jerri. I still think you're wasting your time. Join the force and be a real detective. Of course you'll have to start out on the beat, checking parking meters." Croft gave a superior little laugh.

Jerri laughed, too, but she knew a rookie cop would have to start at the bottom of the heap, and she wasn't much interested in that. Still, it was gratifying to have had two different jobs more or less offered in one day. She must be doing something right. She took Mrs. Page down to the dog pound to pick up Lothario, and received her fee.

One success that didn't come was being hired at Mayhew. Tony phoned and told her he was working on it, but it hadn't been arranged yet. "With their business falling off, the only person they plan to hire is a janitor," he said.

"I'll take it!" she exclaimed at once.

A surprised ring of laughter echoed in her ear. "Do we have a bad connection? I said janitor, as in mopping floors, emptying wastebaskets, cleaning washrooms . . ."

"It's perfect! It would give me an excuse to be all over the plant," she pointed out, undeterred by the menial nature of the work.

"That wasn't the kind of job we discussed," he hedged.

"Besides, the person they're looking for would work the night shift, and go on duty at six P.M."

"That's even better!" Jerri insisted. "I'd have the place virtually to myself to search. And it would mean I could hack a cab or be in my office during the day, too," she added.

"Aren't you forgetting the small matter of sleep?"

"Oh, I can sleep any time," she said dismissively.

"I admire your enthusiasm. Let me talk to Mrs. Mayhew and see if we can't find something better—a position that would give you access to more information," he explained.

But the more she thought of it, the better that particular job seemed. A janitor would have keys to all the offices. She called Tony later that afternoon to point this advantage out to him, but couldn't convince him. Since it was beyond her power to give herself the job, she eventually accepted defeat and called Mike McCane. He didn't require her services that day, so she spent a couple of hours practicing her typing, to be ready for whatever her new role was when it came.

Tony couldn't see her that evening since he had an appointment with Dallyn and the new engineer he was bringing in. She suggested that she should attend the meeting, too, for background information.

"It'll be too technical. These guys are engineers, Jerri," Tony explained. "There's no point wasting your time. I'm sure you've got other cases you're working on."

Pride prevented her from admitting she didn't have a single case to her name, and in the end it was arranged that Tony would call her the next day.

Jerri was beginning to doubt that he would call. In fact, she suspected that Tony had no intention of letting her go to

Mayhew to snoop around. He was just putting her off till the case was finished. But she was pleasantly surprised when the phone at her apartment rang at ten o'clock that night, interrupting her studies of electronic devices.

"I just got back from Glen Williams," Tony said. "Elsa tells me her company is looking for a switchboard operator. Theirs is leaving in two weeks, and they're willing to train someone. Are you interested?"

"Are you kidding? Of course I'm interested! I'll take it."

"Then I suggest you get yourself over to the personnel office early in the morning and apply for the job."

"But it might take a week before they hire me," she objected.

"No, they want someone to start immediately. Just let me check with Elsa," he added. She could hear his voice, farther from the mouthpiece now, and was surprised to learn he was actually with Elsa Mayhew. Where could they be? He was back from Glen Williams. "Yes, they want the replacement to start right away—tomorrow, if possible," he confirmed.

"Good, I'll be there," she replied, but her mind was still half occupied with other thoughts. "Where are you, Tony? Are you in Leamington?" she asked. It was only ten o'clock, not too late for him to come over to the apartment.

"Yes, I'm back, but I'll let you get to bed early, so you'll be ready for the interview tomorrow. Sleep tight, Geraldine."

"Thanks Tony. Goodnight." She hung up the phone slowly, wearing a puzzled frown.

He hadn't been very informative about his whereabouts. Was he at Elsa's house? Was Elsa at the Everett Hotel with him? He had never called Mrs. Mayhew "Elsa" before.

And hadn't she heard music in the background? A business meeting wouldn't go on so late, and shouldn't have musical accompaniment. Suddenly she felt uneasy. She thought of Elsa Mayhew, looked at her from a man's point of view, and the unease heightened. Elsa was attractive. She wasn't a day under thirty-seven, but Tony was nearly thirty himself. They'd have a lot in common, both being in the same business.

The more she thought of it, the more she disliked it. She had to know where he was. She looked up the phone number of the Everett Hotel, dialed and placed a call for Mr. Lupino. If he was there, she'd ask what time Mayhew opened for business—any excuse would do. But he wasn't in his room. At Elsa's house then, at ten-fifteen at night . . . alone with her. Bill Dallyn certainly hadn't driven in from Glen Williams, and she couldn't see any reason why the newly hired engineer would be there either. No, it wasn't business being discussed at this hour. It was something else, and she had a pretty good idea what that something else was.

"Damn!" she said, and punched the pillow on the sofa. Then she went to bed, somewhat depressed.

By morning she'd decided to concentrate on the job and her mood changed to one of anticipation. She dressed in a crisp business suit, pulled her hair back in a tidy chignon, and then drove out to the Mayhew plant. The director of personnel wore a conspiratorial look, but didn't say anything to indicate his complicity in the hiring. By ten o'clock she'd filled in the necessary forms and was installed behind a massive switchboard with the present operator, Nancy Dewar, learning the mysteries of the system. It was a modern, push-button board, with lights flashing rapidly as calls came in and calls were placed. By noon, Jerri's head was swimming, but she'd grasped the rudiments.

"I go to lunch from twelve to one," Nancy told her. "The board won't be busy at noon hour. Do you think you can handle it alone?

"I don't know," Jerri answered truthfully. "But I'll give it my best shot."

The noon hour was quiet. A few local calls were placed, but there were no troublesome long-distance ones. In her spare time, Jerri read the instruction manual. She was looking forward to one o'clock, when she'd be on her lunch hour and could go to the cafeteria to begin meeting some people. She certainly wasn't learning much anchored behind a switchboard.

At one, Nancy returned and Jerri found her way to the cafeteria. It was nearly empty, since the general lunch break was from twelve to one. The mailboy, a bright-eyed teenager named Ed, came to sit with her. He was full of information, but none of it was very useful. It consisted of some plant gossip, but mostly focussed on personal plans to work his way up to the presidency of the company by the time he was thirty-five.

At two, Jerri went back to the switchboard for three more hours of work. She felt fairly competent to handle it when Nancy took her coffee break at three. She'd decided that her best chance of learning anything was to listen in on calls from the engineering department, when time permitted. She listened in on four or five calls, but as Tony had said of the meeting the night before, the talk was too technical to be meaningful to her.

By five, her head was aching. She knew lights would be flashing all night in her dreams. "What do we do about the board at five?" she asked Nancy.

"We connect these three lines," Nancy explained. "One's in the secretarial pool, one's in the cafeteria, and one's in Mr. Wainwright's office. He's the chief engineer." As she spoke, she set up the lines. "That's in case anyone is working overtime. The office staff uses the secretarial pool's line, the factory workers use the cafeteria phone, and the engineers use Mr. Wainwright's line."

"You'd think it would be more convenient to leave one of the other phones in the Engineering Department connected," Jerri mentioned, her mind already active. "That way, the engineers wouldn't have to go trooping into Mr. Wainwright's office."

"That's the way Mr. Wainwright wants it, and you don't argue with the big shots. He usually works nights. Frankly, things are a mess in his department," Nancy said. "When he has staff working overtime, he lets me know, and I give them another line."

"I see," Jerri said, nodding. "I'm going to stick around for a while and read the manual."

"You're really enthusiastic!" Nancy laughed, and picked up her purse. "Remember, don't disconnect those three lines. You can just ignore the rest of the board. You don't have to take any calls after five. That's quitting time. See you tomorrow."

" 'Bye."

The office workers left by the main door near the switchboard. Jerri watched them go, some eagerly, some slowly. The few she had met nodded or spoke, but most of them just went by without a look. When Ed, the mailboy, came by, he stopped to talk.

"How are you making out, Jerri?" he asked.

"It's all very confusing the first day," she answered, smiling at him. She had a plan that involved Ed, and counted on his fairly obvious attraction to her to execute it. "Once I learn my way around, it'll be easier. Nobody gave me a tour of the place."

"Personnel should have done that. They probably will tomorrow."

"I don't think so. I can't leave the board, you see. I thought I'd meander around the halls now. Where do you suggest I start?"

"Why don't I show you around?" he offered promptly. "I know this place inside out. That's my job. I go to every desk in the company."

"Would you mind?" she asked, hopefully.

"I'd be glad to," he said, and held open the half gate that cut her off from the traffic.

True to his word, Ed knew every desk in the company, and with careful questioning, told Jerri what he knew of the occupants. She was particularly interested in the engineering department. The executive offices were ranged around three sides of a large area, where the staff engineers worked at rows of desks separated by bookcases and filing cabinets. Three men were still at their desks, and she wondered if Tony's man was one of them.

"I suppose you know all their names?" she asked Ed.

"I don't recognize the tall guy with red hair," Ed admitted. "He must be new here."

That must be Tony's engineer then. She looked at him for

a minute, trying to catch his eye, hoping for a chance to introduce herself, but he took no notice. It was strange that he hadn't found some opportunity to approach her. He must have heard from Tony that she was here, wanting to help.

"Which is Mr. Wainwright's office?" she asked.

"That's it with the light on," Ed said, pointing across the room to the only executive office with a light still on, indicating he was still hard at work. The other doors were closed, but this wasn't the time to see if they were actually locked. A locked door struck her as a suspicious thing, but not so suspicious as the fact that Mr. Wainwright put in so much overtime. She regretted again that she couldn't have come in as the night janitor. It would have made her job easier.

When the tour was finished, she gave Ed a lift downtown and thanked him. Before going home, she stopped at her office to pick up the mail and check the phone messages. The phone bill had arrived and a few pieces of junk mail, but there were no recorded messages. A couple of calls had come in, but no one had left a message on the machine. She really should have a secretary. Maybe she'd hire a young man, somebody who could help her with the rougher end of the business. She unlocked her desk drawer to make sure that Joe's gun was still there, safe and sound. It was so menacing that she didn't even like to look at it.

It occurred to her that Ed, the mailboy, was a bright young fellow. He might be interested to exchange the presidency of the company for a job as a private investigator. But it would be a mean trick to play on him. It really wasn't a very good career. Since Joe's death, she hadn't enjoyed it much at all. She sat down and thought about her future. Where was she going? Was she going to continue this piecemeal kind of existence for the rest of her life, like Joe? The "wave of the future" definitely bored her. She used any excuse to put off studying the electronics text. Maybe it was time she cut her losses and tried some other line of work.

Her hectic hours at the board that day hadn't allowed her much time to think of Tony, but now that she was free, his image surfaced. Behind it loomed the less happy vision of Elsa Mayhew. There was no message from Tony on the machine. She sighed wearily, and rubbed her tired neck. How had she gotten so tired, just sitting all day? She felt as if she'd run a marathon. Even her legs ached. It must be from sitting at the cramped switchboard.

When a shadow loomed on the frosted glass of her door, she was looking abstractedly out the window, and didn't see it. The turning knob alerted her to company. She turned her head and looked, hopeful of seeing a customer.

"Tony!" she exclaimed, beaming. She quickly forgot her fatigue, her cramped muscles, and the uncertainty of her future. For the moment, she even forgot Elsa Mayhew. Just one glimpse of his flashing smile and she felt happy all over.

"Bearing a gift," he said, stepping in and handing her a can of root beer. "They were out of Coke. You can exchange it for my ginger ale if you prefer."

"Root beer's fine," she said, accepting it. A cold drink was exactly what she wanted. She hadn't had a soft drink all day.

"How'd it go?" Tony asked, taking a perch on the edge of her desk and pulling the tab on his can. "You look frazzled, poor thing."

"It was fairly futile. I may have a line on something

though. I think Mr. Wainwright behaves a little suspiciously.''

"Wainwright? Oh, you don't have to worry about
George. Bill Dallyn hand-picked him for his successor.
Wainwright's clean,'' Tony said firmly.

"Oh.'' She felt a sense of letdown. "What did your
engineer discover? And what's his name anyway? I thought
he'd look me up some time today.''

"Nick Charleston. No, actually I think it would be better
if you two seem not to know one another, just in case our
target is suspicious. Nick's been taken on as a special
assistant to Wainwright.''

"We could arrange to meet accidentally,'' Jerri suggested. "It's foolish not to be working together. Why don't
you ask him to call me at least? On the switchboard, I mean.
No one would know who he's talking to.''

"But would you have time for a personal call?'' Tony
asked.

"I'd make time.''

"I'll suggest it to him, but Nick's pretty busy. He's
doing some spade work. The problems that are plaguing
Mayhew started a few years ago, so he's going over old
material,'' Tony said vaguely. He looked out the window,
almost as though he weren't interested in this discussion.

When she replied, her voice was testy. "He has the
advantage of knowing what he's looking for.''

Tony looked surprised at her reaction. "You're the one
who pressured me into getting you the job, Jerri. You and
Nick aren't in competition to see who wins. What would be
the point of your discussing technical matters with Nick?
Let him do his job, and if you overhear anything interesting
on the board, tell me, and I'll pass it along.''

"I could just pass it along directly to him by phone," she pointed out.

"Sure, that'll be even more efficient. Hmmm, I think I know your problem. You're suffering withdrawal symptoms. I bet you haven't had a fix of pizza or tacos all day. Am I right?"

"Yes, you're absolutely right," she agreed, and was suddenly aware of a gnawing hunger. "The cafeteria food is awful—mayonnaise-soaked sandwiches and weak coffee."

"Elsa said they serve hot meals," he said, surprised.

"They do, if you call two soggy fishsticks and a spoonful of coleslaw a meal. Oh, and french fries, hard as rocks."

"I guess Elsa has never eaten there," he said.

"How are you and Elsa getting along? Does she seem interested in your buying her out?" Jerri tried to keep her voice businesslike, but her eyes betrayed her interest. She studied Tony's face closely for a clue to his feelings.

"She's a little reluctant to give up her husband's company. She suggested a partnership," he mentioned.

"Does the idea of a partnership with Elsa appeal to you?" she asked, still examining him. It immediately occurred to her that Elsa might be using it as an excuse to entangle Tony in her web. She'd never thought of Elsa as a black widow spider-type before, but since last night, she was rapidly becoming one.

"I prefer to run the show myself," Tony replied, failing to read anything personal in Jerri's questions. "Of course if I could romance her into a forty/sixty split, with myself holding the sixty, I'd have the controlling interest at less cost."

"*Romance* her?" she asked, pouncing on the word. "Isn't that an unusual way of doing business?"

"Yes, but then it's unusual for a woman to be the owner of a large company. I know she's an acquaintance of yours, so I'll watch my tongue, but if the wine and candlelight I was treated to last night weren't designed to appeal to my chivalrous instincts, I'd be greatly surprised."

Jerri had considerable trouble keeping her temper under control on hearing this speech. It was Elsa Mayhew she was furious with, but Tony was the one sitting with her, and he bore the brunt of her outburst. "Candlelight and wine! My, that does sound romantic. Elsa is still quite attractive, of course, for an older woman."

Tony tilted his head and laughed. "I suppose thirty-five seems old to a youngster like you."

"If we're still discussing Elsa, it seems incredibly young for her," she answered blandly, though even while she was uttering the jealous remark she regretted it.

"She's in her prime. Come on, I'll feed you before you turn into a cat before my very eyes." He put out his hand peremptorily, but she ignored it.

"I didn't call her old. I said older."

"Older than what, Methuselah?"

"Older than I am, or you for that matter," she said, trying to extricate herself from the charge of cattiness.

"We agree she's well seasoned. Now can we go?" he asked impatiently. "I have an appointment at seven-thirty."

"With Elsa?" she asked, throwing him a glance from the corner of her eyes.

"No, no. She's much too dangerous for a stripling like me. My appointment is with dull businessmen, some of my staff who are working on this Mayhew thing."

"Why don't I join you?" she suggested, but knew he'd claim it was all too technical for her.

"You're perfectly welcome to spend the evening in my bedroom at the hotel if you like—that's where we're meeting—but why don't you wait till my associates have left?"

She tried to read the expression in his dark eyes, and couldn't decide whether he was laughing at her, or if he meant it.

"Actually I have some staff coming from New York, he continued. It'll take quite a while to go over accounting and legal matters."

This removed the onus of having to acknowledge his ambiguous invitation, till he added provocatively, "But they'll be leaving about eleven, I imagine. Then I'll be free, and very happy to see you.

"A tempting suggestion," she answered sarcastically, "but I have to be up at seven-thirty in the morning. Shall we go and eat?"

She locked her office and they went out into the street. As Tony walked in the direction of a brown Chevy that was parked near the corner, Jerri exclaimed, "You've rented a car!"

"I had to. My favorite taxi driver isn't driving these days. I don't hitch a ride in just any old cab, you know. I'm a one-cab man."

They drove to the Pizza Parlor, but the parking lot was crowded, so Tony cruised on through town. "Every place is busy at this hour," Jerri cautioned. "We could try the drive-through window at that hamburger place."

"Delightful. Will it be a cheeseburger with the works for

you? I'm into fried chicken myself,'' he said, turning into the parking lot.

"Dull and unimaginative,'' she scoffed. "I'll have the ribs, and an order of french fries.''

"Coke?''

"No, a chocolate shake. I only had half a soggy sandwich for lunch.''

"You give a new meaning to the word food, Geraldine,'' he said, shaking his head.

"It's fast, and you're in a hurry,'' she reminded him.

When the food cartons were deposited in her lap and the car parked in the lot, they both ate with relish. The meat was falling off the ribs, juicy and tender, and the fries were crisp. The milk shake was so thick she could hardly get it through her straw.

"How's your chicken?'' she asked.

"Edible.''

"You should have taken the sweet and sour sauce. It's fantastic. I've never tried the barbeque.'' She looked with interest at his food.

"I know a hint when I hear one. Here, glutton,'' he said, dipping a piece of chicken into the sauce and popping it into her mouth.

"What are you doing tonight?'' Tony asked after a moment.

"It looks like the old electronics book for me,'' she answered, but with no enthusiasm. "It teaches you how to use bugging devices, how alarm systems work, how to spot if a telephone's been tapped and things like that. It's all very useful,'' she said dutifully, and didn't add that it was also extremely dull, to her, at least.

"Do you really like your job?" he asked, pushing the straw into his drink.

"It's like any job; parts of it are boring. Parts are exciting. I imagine even doctors get bored after a while, setting broken bones and taking out tonsils."

"Sure, when you've seen one inflamed tonsil, you've seen them all," he agreed. "What are the exciting parts of your work?"

"I like helping people. It was fun finding Mrs. Page's dog, and when I first started, Joe and I used to trace kids that had left home. I haven't had one of those cases lately," she said, rather wistfully.

"Surely there are more interesting ways of helping people," he suggested. "You seem well-educated."

"Well, but not properly for social work, if that's what you're thinking of. And I'm a little old to start studying to be a doctor or a lawyer or something like that. I frittered away my youth, studying literature and painting and stuff like that."

"I think you still have a few years of youth left in you," he said, and touched her chin. "Did you pick up any languages in your travels? You seemed pretty familiar with French the other night."

"My Italian's better actually, but I don't see how I could use it for a job."

"You mentioned having frittered away your youth. How much time have you actually invested in being a private investigator?"

"A few years, but not full time. I drive a cab, too, don't forget. Why do you ask?" She looked at him, curious to learn if he had a suggestion.

"You're bright, well-traveled, have a knowledge of a few languages, along with your more obvious assets," he added, trailing his eyes over her.

"I'm afraid to ask what these obvious assets are," she said hesitantly.

"Forget them then. You're still marketable."

"You must be talking about the tourist industry. I'm not interested in leading bunches of tourists around the galleries of Europe. I've been there. I want to settle down. That's the only reason—I mean the main reason why I came to Leamington."

"Being with your father must have been the main reason, and he's no longer here, Jerri." She rather expected some sympathy, but he didn't offer any. He just looked at her, with questioning eyes.

"My aunt and uncle are still here," she answered.

"I don't hear you talk about them much. Are you particularly close to them?"

"Outside of Mom, they're the only family I have left. I'd see Mom more often if I were a tourist guide, I suppose," she added, settling her chin in her fist to concentrate.

"I wasn't talking about the tourist business," he said mildly.

"What did you have in mind then?" While she waited for an answer, she put the straw of her shake in her mouth and drew in the remaining liquid, till a rattling sound told her she had hit bottom.

He took the empty carton from her and put it in the bag. "Oh, nothing specific. There are all kinds of jobs out there if you know where to look for them. Public relations, things like that."

"Yeah, maybe I should start looking," she agreed, but with little conviction.

Tony drove her back to her office to pick up her car. Since the public parking place didn't allow them any privacy, Tony helped her into her car and just squeezed her fingers, saying, "Take care of yourself, Geraldine. I'll call you tomorrow."

"Okay. Thanks for dinner."

"That wasn't dinner," he laughed. "I bet you'll drop by the pizza place on the way home and see if the crowd has dispersed yet."

"No, but I do plan to stop at the ice cream parlor for a cone," she admitted.

He shook his head sadly. "You'll turn into a baby blimp if you keep this up." Then he lowered his head to the window and gave her a fleeting kiss. "But go ahead, it'll be all the more of you to love." He waved and walked away, while she was still savoring that unexpected word, "love."

She watched his car disappear down the street, while she sat at the wheel, thinking. "All the more of you to love." It was just a joke, of course. People shouldn't joke about something as precious as love. Was it possible he wasn't joking?

Chapter Eight

Jerri found that her job at Mayhew was about the worst job she could have, as far as the investigation was concerned. She was tied to the switchboard all day, and it was so busy that she couldn't even listen in on calls, which was her only way of learning who the culprit might be. She was determined to put her lunch hour to good use.

When she had reached the cafeteria and selected an uninspired bowl of chili and an order of toast for lunch, she looked around the tables for the most occupied one to begin making some contacts. There were half a dozen people at one table, and she walked toward it. But before she got there, she changed her mind. One of the engineers she had seen working late the night before sat alone, frowning over a long sheet of paper. It wasn't the redhead, Nick Charleston, but a thin, dark-haired young man.

"Hi, do you mind if I join you?" she asked, and put her tray down before he could object.

He looked surprised, but quite happy. "Not at all. Please do."

"You looked so preoccupied, I was afraid maybe you wanted to be alone. Working during your lunch hour, are you?" she asked, glancing at the paper on the table.

"I manage to keep busy," he replied. "I've seen you at the switchboard, haven't I?"

"Yes, I'm replacing Nancy Dewar. What do you do here at Mayhew, Mr. . . . ?"

"Oldham. Brian Oldham. I'm an engineer."

She told him her name and they shook hands. "Have you run into some problem?" she asked leadingly.

"Oh it's an old problem," he said, and explained what she already knew about the faulty motors.

"And you're looking for the problem on that sheet you have there, are you?" she asked, delighted that the whole conversation had come about so naturally.

"Yes, it's just possible some error occurred in copying out this spec. A very minor change in the dimension of any critical part of the motor—it's just micromillimeters I'm talking about—would be enough so that when the metal expands with heat when in use, the engine could malfunction," he explained.

"Boy, somebody will be in big trouble. Who do you think could have done it?" she asked.

"The engineer who drew up the spec sheet, but the project leader should have caught it. A guy named Hollis was the leader when this was done, but he's left. If there's been an error, I expect Hollis will take the blame, whether he's actually responsible or not."

"Because he's not here, you mean?" she asked.

"The absent are usually the ones found guilty," he agreed. "Any of the project leaders who followed Hollis on the job should have caught it, for that matter. Half the trouble is that we've had a lot of turnover on this job. Wainwright kept replacing engineers, trying to discover the fault, you know."

"And are you in charge now?" she asked.

"I'm in the unhappy position of having some responsibility for the motor, without the authority to put a moratorium on its production till the trouble is sorted out. It's crazy to go on selling a bad engine."

"Why do they do it?" she asked.

"For money, to keep up the cash flow. It's very shortsighted, it'll only wreck the plant's reputation. I wish Wainwright would stop production," he said, rubbing his head.

"Is he the man who has the ultimate say on it?" she asked.

"I guess so. He's the chief engineer."

And Tony said Wainwright was definitely clean, so where did that leave them? She'd learned what she could from Brian Oldham, so they discussed other matters until two, at which time Jerri returned to the switchboard.

At five, Nancy suggested that Jerri set the board up for the night, to make sure she knew how to do it properly. When it was done, they both left, but Jerri only went to the washroom. She returned to the board after the mass exodus of workers had taken place. She meant to monitor the line from the engineering department. Anyone making a call from there would have to use Wainwright's line.

Nothing interesting happened for a little while. A few

men called home to their wives, and one younger engineer tried three times to get a date for the night, finally succeeding with someone called Stacey. By six, the line was silent, and had been for half an hour. Jerri decided to take a walk through the engineering department before she left, just to see who was working late. There was no one in the open space, and the only light on was Wainwright's, who was apparently not under suspicion. She thought it must have been inconvenient for him having all those engineers trooping in to use his phone.

She went back to the switchboard to get her jacket and go home. The light from Wainwright's line was on when she got there. Tony's comprehensive assurance that Wainwright wasn't responsible for the trouble hadn't really convinced her. He was in charge of the whole operation. Changing project leaders so often might have been done in an effort to find the problem, but it might just have been to get rid of any engineer who was getting too close to the solution, too. She pushed the button and put the earphone to her ear.

A man's voice was speaking, in a deep and rather nervous tone. "I did just as you told me to. Three of the plant's best customers have canceled. I expect you'll want the evidence out of here. Shall I take the specs to the hotel?"

Jerri's heart lurched painfully. The hair on her arms rose involuntarily in goose bumps. It was Wainwright! And he was talking to the man who'd put him up to this scheme! The evidence! She must learn what was going to be done with it.

"No, we can't be seen together," a voice answered. That short sentence was enough to identify the speaker beyond a doubt. She'd heard Tony's voice often enough to be certain.

Tony Lupino was the man Wainwright was reporting to. A low gasp escaped from her throat, but she had her hand over the mouthpiece, and knew she wouldn't be heard.

"But I've got to have those specs," Tony added.

"We have to talk, Mr. Lupino," Wainwright said.

"Yes, but I don't want you to come here. There's a park at the river front. Nobody will be there after dark. Meet me by the jetty in front of the statue at, say, nine tonight."

"Shall I bring the specs?" Wainwright asked.

"No, mail them to me as soon as you leave. The U.S. Post is the safest place for them tonight. We wouldn't want them to fall into the wrong hands. Does anyone there seem suspicious?"

"I don't think anyone's caught on yet."

"Good. Make sure you're not followed when you come to the park tonight," Tony said. His voice was calm, matter-of-fact. He'd done this sort of thing before. He wasn't even a little ruffled or nervous. Triumph was the only emotion she could distinguish in his voice.

"All right, Mr. Lupino. I'll do that. I think we owe ourselves some congratulations. This will be a very profitable venture for you. And me," Wainwright added, and laughed. "You haven't forgotten my reward?"

"I'll make it well worth your while, as we discussed. See you at nine."

Tony hung up, and Jerri waited till Wainwright had hung up too before flicking off the switch. She sat stunned at what she had learned. Her first reaction of shock and sorrow was rapidly turning to anger. Tony was a liar and a thief, and as she had suspected all along, he'd only stuck her behind a switchboard so she wouldn't be free to really investigate. She realized that her own position could soon be dangerous if Wainwright should leave now and see her at the board. She picked up her jacket and purse and ran out to her car.

She drove straight home, without stopping at her office. What did it matter? She never had any phone messages anyway. She double-bolted and chained her apartment door behind her, a precaution she didn't usually bother with. Leamington had seemed so safe, so free of crime, a private investigator couldn't even make a decent living.

When the phone jangled, she jumped and drew away from it, as though it had struck her. Tony was the first thought that flashed into her mind and she let the phone ring. She couldn't possibly speak to him now. Her agitation would tell him that she knew. Knew he was a crook, come here to steal Elsa Mayhew's plant from her, while pretending to help her. He'd probably been scheming and working on this for years, then bribed Wainwright to change those specs, and purposely driven the Mayhew plant into the ground so he could buy it for a fraction of its value. Then he would step in and correct the faulty engine—so easy since he knew exactly what change to make. He wouldn't give a thought to all the destruction he'd caused, the hundred or so men put out of work, and the suffering of their families. A whole town had been sacrificed for his profit.

And now Wainwright was going to smuggle the specifications out of the plant so no one could ever prove what he'd done. You couldn't prosecute a criminal without evidence. He'd get away with it scot-free. She felt sick with regret and worry. She'd been right about Tony the first time she'd seen him climbing off that plane in his racketeer's costume and dark glasses. She'd known from the start he was no good, and should have stayed away from him. She should never have driven him to Glen Williams, and let herself fall under the spell of his liquid brown eyes and charming manners.

The only reason Tony Lupino had ever had anything to do with her was because she was Joe Tobin's daughter. He was worried that she knew what he was up to, and probably felt he had to keep an eye on her. A new wave of pain broke over her. And had he managed to corrupt Joe as well? No, it was still possible Joe had only been his dupe, as she has been. She refused to believe anything else. She needed someone to cling to, even if it was only the memory of her father.

For a long time she sat, fretting over all this. Why had Tony done it? He was wealthy enough already. He didn't need another factory. It was greed, pure and simple.

She remembered Elsa Mayhew, no longer a rival, but another victim of Lupino's lust for power. To lull Elsa's suspicions he'd lied to Bill Dallyn, and charmed Elsa herself. He was good at that. He'd charmed Jerri without half trying.

How was it possible the fun-loving man who'd gone window-peeking with her, who'd eaten pizza and hamburgers and called her Geraldine in that intimate way, could be so evil? How had she not sensed it when he kissed her? She didn't want to think about Tony's kisses, though. They were too powerful, too appealing. It was just as well he had turned out to be a monster, Jerri thought. She couldn't afford to fall in love with him.

But now she had to do something. She was the only one who knew about him, other than Wainwright, who obviously wouldn't tell. To reveal her suspicions to the besotted

Elsa Mayhew would do no good. What evidence did she
have to offer to the police? That she'd listened in on a phone
conversation? They'd laugh in her face. She needed hard,
solid evidence, and with a little daring and cunning, she
might get hold of it.

She knew where and when he was meeting Wainwright,
and she also knew the evidence was in the mail, which
should arrive at Tony's hotel tomorrow morning. Retriev-
ing it meant she couldn't go to work at Mayhew. Nick
Charleston would probably report that she wasn't there. She
was convinced now the only reason she was there was to
allow Tony to keep track of her doings, so she'd better start
preparing some excuse. If he called again, she'd talk to him.

Another half hour passed in this contemplative manner.
When the phone rang again, she went to it without
trembling, though she was shaking inside.

"Hi, Geraldine. It's Tony. Where have you been? Out
stuffing yourself with tacos, I suppose?" This cheery
greeting nearly undid her. This was the side of him she had
been foolish enough to fall for, and it took all her fortitude
to act her part. Anger and determination forced her to hold
her tongue. This wasn't the time to tell him what she
thought of him.

"Hello, Tony. No, I haven't eaten. If fact, I have a
headache, and a bit of a fever. I think I'm coming down
with something," she added. Her voice bolstered this
claim. It sounded tired and weak from worry.

His quick response was full of concern. "Have you
called a doctor?"

"No, my aunt wants me to go over to her place. It's
probably only a touch of flu or something, but she doesn't

want me to be alone. I don't think I'll be able to go to work tomorrow.'' She waited to hear his response to this, wondering if he suspected anything. His reply reassured her on that score.

"I'm sorry to hear it, sweetheart. Is there anything I can do? Why don't you let me drive you to your aunt's place?''

That spontaneous ''Sweetheart'' fell like thunder on her ear, jarring her, and inciting her to fresh anger at his duplicity. She clenched her hands into fists and fought back her emotions.

"My uncle's coming to pick me up. Thanks anyway, Tony.''

"Will it be possible for me to see you while you're there?'' he asked. Was he becoming suspicious? Why did he suggest that?

"I'll be in bed. I probably won't be able to see anyone. I really feel miserable,'' she said, with perfect sincerity.

"Why don't I come over to your apartment now? I'll stay with you till your uncle arrives,'' he suggested. She looked at the clock. Not even seven o'clock yet. Sure, he'd have plenty of time to see her before meeting Wainwright at nine. She was revolted that he could think of sitting and smiling at her, before going out to scheme and bribe that same evening. She had to get rid of him quickly, before she said something foolish.

"I hear my uncle at the door right now. I'd better go. Thanks for calling.''

"You take good care of yourself. I have plans for you that require you to be in top form,'' he said, in the hearty accents reserved for invalids. Then in a gentle, yearning voice he added, ''I wish I could see you.'' She could well imagine the look in his eyes when he said it. It was imperative that he not see her, certainly not in any intimate circumstances that would permit him to change her mind.

"I have to go now," she said. " 'Bye, Tony."

"I—" He came to a quick stop.

"What?" she asked.

"I love you," he said, and sounded surprised at his own words.

"Oh!" The air caught in her lungs. For an instant she felt suffocated, unable to speak. What did one say to such an admission? She said, "Good-bye," in a voice that shook a little, and hung up quickly.

Her hand rested on the phone. She looked at the receiver, wondering if she had misheard or misunderstood him. He even sounded sincere. She felt a weakening of her resolve, and thought of Joe. It gave her strength to do the right thing. She managed to convince herself that Tony was just romancing her into line.

The story of a headache had begun as a lie, but by the time she'd finished with Tony, it was true. She lay on the sofa and sat staring at the window as the sky slowly darkened from blue to pearly gray. She hadn't eaten anything since the chili at lunch, but she wasn't hungry. She didn't even want a soft drink. She just wanted nine o'clock to come, so she could go to the park and spy. It seemed an eternity that she lay there, reliving her whole life, yet when the clock said eight-thirty, and it was time to prepare to leave, she was surprised it had come so soon. She felt disoriented, confused, and distraught.

Jerri was familiar with the park and the statue honoring the veterans of the First World War. It was an old bronze statue, turning green and gray from exposure, and used by children and seagulls. It had an enormous concrete base, and was surrounded by a hedge of yews which would be a good hiding place for her and be close enough for her to overhear every word Lupino and Wainwright said.

She changed into jeans, running shoes, and a navy blue jacket, and covered her hair in a dark scarf to make herself less visible in the darkness of night. She considered stopping by the office to get her gun, but knowing she wouldn't use it, she didn't bother. She drove past the park to the far end of the jetty so her car wouldn't be seen, then backtracked by foot. At ten to nine, she was crouching in the bushes, waiting for the men to come. It was cold down by the water, and her hunched position was uncomfortable. She was also struck with an awful hunger, but mostly she was frightened, and wished she'd brought the gun after all. What if they saw her? Would they possibly kill her, to conceal their crime?

Wainwright was the first to drive up. At least she assumed it was Wainwright. She couldn't really see the man, just a dark, tall shadow, pacing back and forth along the jetty, beyond the statue. Three minutes later Tony arrived on foot; he'd probably taken a cab to the park entrance since he had only hired the Chevy for the day.

"Ah, there you are!" Wainwright exclaimed, when he spotted Tony.

They both looked up and down the jetty. Although it was free of people, there was a chilly wind blowing. "Shall we go to my car? It's damned cold here," Wainwright said, and the two of them walked toward his car.

A tide of frustration washed over Jerri. What should she do now? There was no cover on the jetty. If she followed them, they'd be sure to see her, yet she couldn't hear a word from here. She peered through the bushes till the shadows swallowed up the men, then she quietly crept out and began to follow. She heard two car doors open and close, and darted quickly forward to see if there was an open window. While she peered through the night, the engine started. Two mocking red tail lights showed, then pulled away, and she was left standing alone on the cold jetty.

"Oh, damn!" she muttered, and stamped her foot in frustration. Now she'd never know what they said. She hurried back to her own car, but by the time she got to the far end of the jetty and drove back to the statue, they were long gone. She knew they wouldn't have gone to the hotel, and didn't think Wainwright's house a likely spot either. They were probably just driving around. A moving vehicle was a good safe place for private, criminal conversations. She couldn't think of anything to do but drive home to her apartment.

The outing in the fresh air had given her a good appetite, and she began cooking to distract her mind. She made bacon, eggs, toast, and coffee, and opened a bottle of red currant jelly. As she was about to begin this feast, the phone rang. She didn't hesitate to answer it this time. Tony wouldn't be calling her here; he thought she was at her aunt's house.

"Jerri, it's Dorothy," the cultivated voice said.

"Oh, hi, Dorothy. How are you?"

"I'm confused. A beautiful bouquet of roses has just arrived here for you. Shall I open the card and see who they're from?" she asked.

"That's not necessary. I know who they're from," Jerri replied grimly.

"Oh, and will you come over to pick them up?"

"You can just dump them in the garbage pail and save me the trip, Dorothy," Jerri said in a tight, angry voice.

"Oh-ho! A lovers' quarrel! But surely you want to see the card at least."

"I don't, but I think you do. Go ahead and open it," Jerri said, and listened with some curiosity to hear the message.

She heard the crackle of the envelope being opened. "It says 'These are for display purposes only, not to be eaten. Get well immediately, Geraldine. All my love, Anthony.' What a strange message. Who's Anthony?"

"He's nobody special. Just a man I met. You can throw the card out, too," Jerri said, but a sad little smile tugged at her lips now.

"My, it must be nice to have so many boyfriends you can treat them like dirt! If you don't want them, I'll keep them. They'll look beautiful—two dozen long-stemmed roses. Just gorgeous, and the smell!"

"What color are they?" Jerri asked, almost against her will.

"A dozen white, and a dozen a beautiful, soft shade of pink. They'd match your living room perfectly. I wonder if Anthony had it in mind when he bought them." This was a not very subtle hint to learn whether Anthony was a frequent guest at the apartment.

"Probably, he was here once."

"Just once?"

"Just once, Dorothy. I'm not involved in a flaming affair," Jerri assured her.

"But why did he send them here, if he knows where you live?"

Not too much slipped past Dorothy's quick mind. "I said

I was visiting you for a few days, so he wouldn't be pestering me here. I hope you don't mind?''

"Happy to oblige you, any time. Is he likely to drop around my place?"

"No, I told him I had the flu. That was my excuse for being with you. If he phones, please tell him I'm too sick to come to the phone.''

"But there's a phone right by the guest bed. But of course he wouldn't know that. How silly of me! Tell me all about him. Is he really that undesirable? What's his last name?''

"He's nobody you'd know, Dorothy. Just a man who's visiting town for a few days," Jerri answered vaguely.

"It wouldn't be Anthony Lupino, would it? No, of course not. It's foolish of me to ask. He's much too respectable to be of interest to you," Dorothy said, a tinge of annoyance creeping into her tone.

"Who's Anthony Lupino?" Jerri asked, feigning ignorance.

"He's a friend of Elsa Mayhew, but of course there's no way you could have met him. I wonder if I could get her to introduce us to him. He's extremely eligible, and much too young for Elsa, no matter what she thinks.''

Jerri smarted under this information. Much as she despised Tony, it hurt to know another woman had plans for him. "I'd better let you go," she said. "You probably have company.''

"There's no hurry. I'm playing bridge and losing my shirt, but perhaps I should get back to the table. Thanks for the roses.''

"You're welcome.''

They hung up, and Jerri returned to her meal. It had

grown cold, but that ordinarily wouldn't have affected her
appetite much if she had felt like eating. Right now, she felt
more like crying. Her heart was heavy in her chest, causing
a dull pain. Heartache, that's what it was. What a perfect
description of her condition. She'd felt the same when Joe
died. She'd felt angry then, too, just as she felt now. Angry
with Fate, for having once again snatched away her happiness. Was she never going to find someone to love, to hold
on to for more than a minute?

She'd done all the right things. She'd turned her back on
her mother's futile lifestyle. She'd settled down and worked
hard, so why was she being tortured by all these misfor-
tunes? She didn't have any lavish desires, just a need to love
and belong to somebody. Was that so much to ask of life?

She scraped her plate into the garbage can, opened a soft
drink and put Ravel on the stereo. To relieve the heartache,
she closed her eyes and imagined she was again in Tony's
arms, waltzing to that deliriously mad music, without a care
in the world except getting dizzy from whirling. She
imagined the pink and white roses, and mentally selected a
spot for them in her living room. There, they'd look best on
the shelf of the highboy. Had he sent roses to Elsa, too, to
keep her in the proper state of infatuation? It was a small
price to pay for ripping her off for thousands of dollars. But
he wouldn't get away with it. She jumped up and turned off
the stereo, and sat down to figure out how to get the
evidence that was in the mail.

She'd be at the Everett Hotel tomorrow when the
specifications arrived, and by hook or by crook she'd get
the envelope. It would be left at the desk, and put in Tony's
mailbox for him to pick up when he came down. The clerk
wouldn't give it to her, obviously, but maybe she could take

it from Tony's box, if she could divert the clerk for a minute.

She'd have to get there early, and take up her post in the lobby with a newspaper held in front of her. She'd play it by ear. The important thing was that she knew it would be there, and Tony didn't know she knew, so he wouldn't be taking any precautions. Once she got the envelope, she'd take it to Elsa and explain the situation to her. She wondered if Bill Dallyn was to be trusted, or if Tony had managed to buy his cooperation as well. In any case, Elsa wasn't a fool. She'd listen when she knew her company was at stake.

There should be a good reward in it for her, too. Elsa hadn't hired her, but common decency would surely impel her to offer some reward. Dorothy would be helpful in dropping a hint if all else failed. And with that and the five thousand from Joe, maybe she'd go to her mother's wedding after all. Or she could use the money to train herself for some other line of work. Investigating wasn't any fun without Joe. In fact, Leamington wasn't any fun without him.

Why had she ever taken up this line of work in the first place? Just to be with her father, that was all. Oh, it was fun to hear Dorothy and her friends and Mike McCane and any sane adult she met tell her it was too dangerous for a woman. She'd rather enjoyed that aspect of it. She sat frowning with the effort of being completely honest with herself. No, what you really enjoyed was the attention, she finally admitted. You never got your fair share of that, with your mother always outdoing you. That's why you left Europe, to get away and create a world where you mattered. And when people worried about your safety, they paid the very best kind of attention. They cared—they wouldn't worry about you if they didn't care.

Well, maybe it was time to grow up and accept that a few people did care about her, and stop worrying them to death by proving it in this line of work. It really wasn't even all that dangerous, the cases she had. She'd take her money and study something useful—nursing, maybe. That would be a worthwhile occupation.

She tried to divert her thoughts with these future plans, but when she finally went to bed and lay alone in the dark, she thought only of Tony. How could he have done it? How could he betray her like this? And why did he go and tell her he loved her, and send her flowers if he only meant to leave her? Would he go to jail? Would she be the one to stand in the witness box and accuse him? It was too awful to think of, but too much in her mind not to think of it. She scarcely slept all night long. At three o'clock she was still wide awake. Her eyes weren't wet; she had gone beyond tears long ago.

Chapter Nine

If a woman wanted to be inconspicuous in the lobby of the Everett Hotel, she didn't wear just any old rags. Jerri dressed carefully the next morning in a conservative blue suit that wouldn't stand out. She realized, as she stood observing herself in the mirror, that her hair would draw attention to her, and pinned it up behind. The face in the mirror looked tired and pale, with purple smudges below the eyes from her sleepless night. She tried on dark glasses, but they'd be too noticeable, especially indoors, so she returned them to her purse. She remembered to phone Mayhew before leaving and tell them she wouldn't be in that day, then drove to the Everett Hotel.

She entered the hotel through the coffee shop to avoid parading past the front desk, where the clerk would probably recognize her. When Tony went looking for his envelope, she didn't want anyone mentioning that she had been there. She bought the morning paper in the coffee shop, and entered the lobby. She chose a chair that gave her a view of the front desk, opened her paper and arranged it to her satisfaction. The nearly empty boxes behind the clerk told her the morning mail hadn't arrived yet.

She sat for fifteen minutes, pretending to read, but constantly peering across to the desk for the mailman. She also glanced over the paper to the elevators, in case Tony came down for breakfast. When the mailman arrived, Tony still hadn't appeared. She watched while the mailman emptied his bag, said a few pleasantries to the clerk, and left. Now was the tricky part. She had to make sure that there was a large envelope in the pile for Tony before doing anything else.

One bit of luck was that she didn't recognize the desk clerk, so presumably he wouldn't recognize her either. She could risk approaching him to get closer to the mail. The clerk was sorting through the letters, sticking them into boxes behind him. She remembered that Tony's room number was 204, and saw two small white envelopes in his box. Neither was large enough to hold specifications from Mayhew. That would require a large envelope.

"Can I help you, ma'am?" the clerk asked, looking up from his work.

"Is there anything there for Miss Julia James?" she asked, inventing a name at random.

"I haven't come across anything yet," he replied, and continued his sorting.

She noticed a large manila envelope in the unsorted pile, and thought it seemed the proper size. When the clerk reached it, she read the name and address. Mr. Anthony

Lupino, Everett Hotel. The evidence was there, at her fingertips, and she longed to snatch it and run. While she quickly considered how to get it from the clerk, he reached for the phone on the counter beside him.

"Mr. Lupino, that envelope has arrived. Shall I send it up?" he asked.

She could hear Tony's reply faintly, although distinctly. "Yes, please. Right away."

"Yes, sir."

Should she offer to take it, say she was going to see Mr. Lupino? But the clerk had obviously been alerted to the envelope's importance, and might not give it to her. She licked her bottom lip nervously and said, "I . . ."

"Excuse me, miss. I'll be right back," the clerk said, and walked swiftly toward the elevator, the envelope in his hand, and a smile on his face as he anticipated his tip.

She took two quick steps after him, but he was too far ahead of her and entered the elevator just as the door was closing. He was gone, and the evidence with him. She'd had it within her grasp, and let it get away. She was disgusted with herself. She'd never get it now. What would Tony do with it? Would he destroy it, burn it up? No, if he'd meant to do that, he'd have had Wainwright burn it at the plant. He must want it for something.

She remembered how he had always carried his briefcase with him when he first arrived in Leamington, and thought that perhaps he would put the specifications in there. If he did, it would never leave his side, and she'd have hard work getting it from him. She went back to her chair and newspaper to think. Maybe she should accost him when he came down. Say she'd felt better, and had taken the day off work to recuperate. She could suggest they go out, do something, and when she got the chance, she'd steal the briefcase and run.

The clerk soon returned to his work, smiling broadly and patting his pocket. It seemed an eternity before Tony came down. He wore a light tan suede jacket and fawn trousers, and looked ravishingly handsome. But more importantly, he wasn't carrying his briefcase. So the envelope was in his room. Her eyes followed him as he entered the coffee shop. He'd probably take twenty minutes or so for breakfast, then go back to his room for the briefcase. All right then, that was long enough. She set aside her newspaper and rose from the chair.

She walked casually into the elevator, pushed the button, and rode up. She looked like any young woman going about her business, but her hands were shaking with nervousness. She followed the posted numbers to the proper hallway and saw two cleaning women with carts blocking the passage. They chatted together over their heaps of laundry, soap, and towels, and she eased past them, on down the hall till she reached 204. Her heart was in her mouth as she reached for the knob. What if Tony had left someone in the room with the briefcase? One of those men he was always meeting with. She tried the door, but of course it was locked. Apparently the room was empty since no one came to the door.

She couldn't possibly pick the lock with two hotel employees in plain view. In fact, she probably couldn't pick it if she had half an hour. It was a lot harder than it looked to open a locked door without a key. Her best bet was to boldly ask the cleaning women to open the door for her. Jerri looked eminently respectable. They might not do it, but it was worth a try.

When one of the women looked at her, Jerri went forward. "I've come up without getting the key from my husband," she said, making an annoyed face. "Could you let me into 204? I have to pick up his briefcase. We've got a taxi waiting."

The women exchanged a glance, looked her up and down, and one of them decided she was a law-abiding citizen. "I guess I could do that," she said, and went to open the door. She accompanied Jerri into the room and watched while she looked all around. Neither the envelope nor the briefcase was there. Had someone been in the room with Tony and left by some other exit than the lobby? She quickly examined the room for clues. There was one glass on the bedside table, with some dregs of what looked like beer in the bottom. No, it seemed as though he'd been alone.

"I don't see it," the cleaning woman said. She didn't sound suspicious—not yet.

"That's strange. Harry must have taken it—my husband's assistant. Well, it's only one envelope he wanted anyway. It must be here somewhere. I'll just have a quick look around."

Jerri walked purposefully toward the desk, opened the stationery drawer, knowing it wasn't there, but hesitating to arouse curiosity by rooting under the mattress and in other peculiar places. "If you want to go on with your work, I'll lock the door when I leave," Jerri said over her shoulder.

"I'll wait," the woman answered, becoming suspicious now. "We're not supposed to let people into the rooms, actually."

"Of course. You can't be too careful," Jerri said, and went to the clothes closet. Tony had arrived in Leamington with two pieces of luggage. They were both in the closet, but would the cleaning woman take it into her head to phone the front desk if she started tampering with them? The larger was on the floor. She reached for it, brushing against his navy blazer as she did so. There was a little rustling sound, and a folded manila envelope fell from the sleeve of it. It was hard to contain the shout of pleasure that bubbled up inside her. She quickly composed a calm face and emerged from the closet, clutching the envelope.

"I found it," she said. A tip was definitely in order, but not too large a tip, or it would look odd. Jerri fished a dollar out of her purse, thanked the cleaning woman, and left, her heels clicking as she hastened to the elevator. She didn't look to the right or left as she went through the lobby and out the front door. She drove home, parked the car, and took the envelope into her apartment. She was trembling like a leaf, and felt none of the triumph that usually accompanied a successful case. She was careful to lock the door behind her.

The envelope wasn't sealed so she drew out the papers and looked at them. They were completely meaningless to a layman. They looked like a set of draftsman's careful drawings of machinery, with many gears and small parts whose names she couldn't begin to fathom. There were measurements written in, which she concluded were the clues that would tell an engineer the treacherous story when he compared them to the original designs. Yes, as she studied and compared similar drawings, she noticed some of the numbers were slightly different. But as Brian Oldham had explained, very small changes were enough to ruin precision machinery.

Jerri slid the plans back into the envelope and looked up

Elsa Mayhew's telephone number to tell her she wanted to see her. Elsa's maid answered.

"I'm sorry, Mrs. Mayhew is out this morning."

"It's very important. Could you tell me where I could reach her?" Jerri asked.

"She only said she'd be back for lunch. I believe she's doing some shopping. Could I have her call you?"

"I—I'm not sure I'll be in all morning. I'd better call her back. Thank you." Jerri hung up the phone and sat, undecided. She wanted to finish this unsavory business, and sat pondering who she should call. Bill Dallyn? Who was to say he was innocent. The police? It would be Elsa's place to do that. This really wasn't Jerri's business at all. She had only stumbled into it by chance.

And to add to her indecision, she really didn't want to report Tony at all. She didn't want to take the irrevocable step that would put him in jail. Why had he done it? That was the question that went through her mind again and again. He didn't need the money. He was rich. Rich and greedy, a cunning thief who not only robbed but reached out his tentacles to ensnare others in his guilt. Maybe if she spoke to him, threatened to expose him if he didn't rectify the harm he had done. . . . But that wasn't feasible, and she knew it. He'd only go off and find another victim. Criminals had to be brought to justice, as a professional in her line of work knew perfectly well.

She felt frightened, alone in her apartment, and thought of places she could go to await Elsa's return. She could go to Dorothy's house, or to Elsa's. She might as well go directly to Elsa's, and wait for her there. Jerri picked up the manila envelope reluctantly, as though it were a dead fish. She picked up her car keys, looked around for her purse

which she'd tossed on the sofa when she came in. Was there
anything else? Purse, keys, envelope. She swallowed
twice, straightened her shoulders, and headed for the door.

Before she reached it, she heard the thud of hurried
footsteps ascending the stairs. Don't panic! It's probably
only Mr. Fischer back from his morning walk. But Mr
Fisher was an elderly, retired gentleman. His footsteps
weren't so firm, so fast. It was Tony! He'd discovered her
trick and come after her. Don't panic, she thought again.
The door's locked. He can't get in. He doesn't know you're
here. He'll just knock a few times and leave. Even while
she thought this, there was a pounding at the door.

My car! He's seen my car in the parking lot and knows
I'm here. But I told him my uncle was driving me to
Dorothy's house, so that would explain it. It's probably no
Tony at all. Some darned salesman. This reassuring thought
was interrupted by the unmistakable sound of Tony Lu
pino's voice. "Open up, Jerri. I know you're in there."

She stood perfectly still, clutching the envelope, while
her heart hammered in her chest, echoing in her ears,
depriving her of rational thought.

"Let me in or I'll break the door down!" he threatened,
and the heaving of the door on its hinges gave some
credence to his announcement.

Her main concern was for the envelope. That's what he
was after, but he wouldn't get it. First she looked around for
a means of escape, but there was no convenient fire escape
to help her, and a leap from the window to the concrete
below was out of the question. Next she needed to find a
safe hiding place for the envelope. The first places he'd
look would be under the sofa cushions and the carpet; she
had to do better than that. Her mind racing, she darted into

the bedroom, while behind her the thumps on the door continued, increasing in ferocity. Why didn't someone come to help her? Was she going to be attacked in her own home? But Mr. Fischer would probably be out on his walk, and her other neighbors would be at work.

She looked around the bedroom, choosing her spot. Her choices were woefully few in this small room. The bed, the carpet, the dresser, behind the curtains, in the clothes closet. She wasn't satisfied with any of them, but the pounding on the door continued, lending a desperate urgency to her actions. She looked at the mirror over her dresser—it was large and gilt-framed. Maybe if she stuffed the envelope behind the mirror . . . Her fingers shook, and the rasping sounds of cracking wood warned her the lock was giving way under Tony's forceful blows. She stuck the envelope behind the mirror and darted back into the living room.

First the wood around the doorknob splintered and the door opened two inches, still held shut by the chain. It wasn't ten seconds after that that ineffectual chain was yanked from the wall, and the door was flung wide open. Tony Lupino stood in the doorway, his face red with rage and exertion. But it wasn't his color so much as his murderous expression that chilled the blood in her veins. Those furious eyes turned her to stone. The few seconds he stood glaring seemed a small eternity.

He took two stiff-legged strides into the room and threw the door shut behind him. Free of its lock, it banged back idly. He glared at her and said, "The game's over. Give me the papers," in a voice she wouldn't have recognized as his, if he hadn't stood before her. It sounded like the accents of an executioner.

She tried to answer, but no words came out. It was like a nightmare, with her dry, silent throat adding to her terror. At last she emitted a strained, unnatural sound. "What papers?" she asked, but her white face and rigid posture betrayed her knowledge.

"The envelope you took from my room not half an hour ago. I have enough witnesses to have you arrested. Make it easy on yourself and hand it over." Tony's voice was under control now, low but very menacing. His calmness frightened her. He was a hardened criminal—what wouldn't he do to anyone who thwarted him? But surely someone had heard the racket he made breaking in. Someone would come to see what was the matter.

She clung to this hope and answered, "I don't know what you're talking about."

His eyes glittered cold and hard, like black diamonds. "I won't go easy on you because you're a woman," he threatened. "I don't know who you're working for, or how much you hope to make by this stunt, but by God when you cross swords with me, you better be ready to fight to the death."

For a moment, fear prevented her from understanding the full import of what he was saying, but as she grasped his meaning, anger rose up in her. "I didn't do it for money!" she exclaimed. "How dare you accuse me of that. You're the shifty businessman with sharp deals. I've looked into your background, Mr. Lupino!"

"You're well organized. I should have realized you were no amateur." His eyes narrowed in assessment of her, and his flaring nostrils showed contempt. "You have a convincing act, lady, with your hamburgers and ragged jeans, but you should have stuck to them. Struggling private detectives don't wear designer gowns and live in apartments that look like some anteroom of the Petit Trianon. Why did you invite me up to your lair?''

"I didn't invite you!" she snapped back. "You insisted."

"You don't have to tell me why you agreed. I was waltzed around your living room to soften me up for the kill." His head gave a disparaging toss toward the room as he spoke. "I knew you planned to do some gentle arm twisting to weasel your way into Mayhew, but I was fool enough to mistake you for an idealist, wanting to finish the job your father started for me."

"He never would have worked for you if he'd known what you were up to!" she accused.

"And what was I up to, Miss Tobin?" he demanded, glaring at her.

"You were trying to rob Elsa Mayhew," she answered without hesitation.

She watched, transfixed, as a frown creased his brow, then darkened to a black scowl. "While you, a knight in shining armor, sprang to her defense, out of the goodness of your black little heart? The innocent act won't work a second time. I may be susceptible to women, but I'm not a fool," he scoffed.

"I never thought for a minute you were. Your reputation as a sharp operator is pretty well established in more than one state," she retaliated.

"Who is your informant? Was it your father?"

"No! Leave Joe out of this!"

"Who then?" His hand shot out and he grabbed her wrist in a painful grip. "I'd like to believe you're only somebody's dupe." For one brief instant their eyes met and locked. She was terrified at the anger she saw in his, and surprised at the other emotion, something that looked like pain.

"I'm nobody's dupe," she said, staring in fascination, trying to confirm what she thought she had seen.

"No?" His tone was grimly ironic. "Was *I* the dupe then? You knew all along, when you were conveniently waiting for me at the airport, who I was, and why I was here. You devised the scheme all by yourself to steal the specs and blackmail Wainwright with them." All she could do was look at his eyes. They were on fire with anger and frustration.

She took a deep breath to calm herself and answered in a steady voice, "I wasn't blackmailing anyone. If I were after money, which I'm not, I think we both know who has a lot more of it than Wainwright."

"If you didn't have blackmail in mind, then perhaps you'd condescend to tell me why you *did* interfere in my life? Why the waiting cab at the airport? Why the coy smiles and suggestion I call you if I needed a lift? Why the low-cut dress and the Ravel, Miss Tobin? Those weren't the acts of a disinterested observer. You were after me the minute I hit this town."

"I never pursued you, if that's what you're implying," she said stiffly.

"Oh, I'm well aware of who was allowed to do the pursuing. You let me chase you till you caught me. But it still doesn't make any sense unless you planned to turn a quick profit on it. You found out from Joe what was going on, and put the information to good use after he wasn't around to keep an eye on you. You either planned to sell these papers to Wainwright so he could cover his crime, or to me, so I could catch him. It was either blackmail or extortion and both are criminal acts,'' he informed her. His face looked as though it were carved from ice.

She was overcome by the extreme nature of these charges, by the way he was twisting everything around. She even began to fear she might end up in prison. Her face blanched and she tried to back away from him, but he held on to her wrist in a painful iron grip. ''I don't know what you're talking about. It's not true, none of it.''

He leaned his head closer, and stared at her with a mocking face. ''Is it not true you were at the Everett Hotel this morning either? That you rifled my room and carried off my property?''

''I . . .'' She moistened her lips nervously. ''I don't know what you mean,'' she insisted. She was confused with regard to what exactly was going on at Mayhew, but nothing he'd said so far convinced her he was completely innocent. He might speak of her blackmailing Wainwright, but it was Tony who had bribed Wainwright to bring him the specifications. There was no confusion at all about that. And he'd told her Wainwright was ''clean.''

''The hell you don't,'' Tony growled, and pounced into the living room to search, dragging her behind him, still holding on to her wrist. First the pillows were thrown from her sofa. With one hand, he lifted the end of the sofa and heaved it aside as though it were just another cushion. He leaned over and pulled back the corner of the carpet, revealing the innocent underpad. He continued his course around the room, shaking curtains, pulling out drawers of the highboy and tossing them aside. His hand swiped one of her porcelains off the surface of the highboy as he moved, and it hit a chair. It was the Minton shepherdess her mother had given her for her sixteenth birthday. The delicate neck snapped, and the miniature head of the shepherdess rolled across the floor.

"Stop it! You're destroying everything!" she shouted, pulling away to try to rescue her broken statuette.

He gave a disinterested look at his work and said, "You can count yourself lucky if that's all I break." His black eyes looked at her own throat as he spoke.

A frisson of fear scampered up her spine at the look in his eyes. After that, she said little, but allowed herself to be pulled along while he scattered her phonograph records on the carpet. "I don't have it," was all she said. She kept looking to the door, hoping someone would come and rescue her.

Without a word, Tony strode into the bedroom and began ransacking it. She took one guilty look at the mirror while his eyes were busy elsewhere, and saw to her horror that a corner of the envelope protruded at the bottom. The envelope had slipped. She immediately looked away before he saw where she was looking. He ripped the comforter from the bed, threw the pillows on the floor, pulled off the sheets, and lifted the corners of the mattress, all with one hand, while she stood watching in mute agony, praying he wouldn't find the envelope. The intentness of his search and his towering rage convinced her he was looking for evidence important enough to lock him up for years.

He was breathing hard when he had finished with her bed. "A little cooperation would make it easier for you," he said, through clenched lips.

She just looked at him, silent. Still holding her wrist, he went to the dresser and began pulling out drawers. Her lingerie tumbled in a heap on the floor, slips and bras and panties strewn amidst nighties and nylons. Then the next drawer, with a rainbow of sweaters added to the heap. Scarves, gloves, ribbons were added as the last drawers were thrown aside. Now panting from exertion, Tony moved inexorably to the vanity. His eyes flashed past the mirror, but miraculously missed seeing the corner of the envelope. She couldn't believe her luck. She regarded his image in the mirror, willing him to start on the vanity drawers.

It was like watching a slow-motion horror film. Slowly, very slowly, his eyes returned to the mirror and shifted down to the corner. Then he looked up and gave one mocking, triumphant smile. He let her wrist drop and reached for the envelope. He opened it and took a quick look at the papers, then shoved them back inside.

Anger and frustration rose in Jerri's breast. He'd won. The Tony Lupinos of the world always won. "I hope you're satisfied," she said, and turned away.

His hand came out and gripped her shoulder, flinging her back to face him. "Not quite. There are a few questions I'd like answered before the police get hold of you. I have to know—are you in this with Wainwright? It's too late to try to protect him. You might be able to do yourself some good if you cooperate." He stared hard, as though he were trying to read her soul.

"I'd hardly be working with any cohort of yours, Mr. Lupino," she answered coldly.

"Wainwright is no cohort of mine. You're in it alone then," he said grimly. She neither confirmed nor denied this, but just looked at him, trying to read his expression. It changed even as she looked. There was a flash of mockery on his saturnine face, perhaps tinged with regret. "You're just a bungling amateur. If you're so confused you don't even know the good guys from the bad, I suggest you stick to chasing dogs, Miss Tobin. You might possibly be able to outwit a mongrel, but you're no match for me. Or Wainwright for that matter."

His words stung her pride, and anger flared up. "I haven't your expertise in the field of criminal cunning, but I recognize a thief when I see one. You're not going to get away with it. I heard you and Wainwright on the phone. *You* may have the papers, but *I* have the information. You'd better run along and consult with your legal boys. You'll be needing them."

A frown settled on Tony's face as he tried to make sense of this utterance. "I've never spoken to Wainwright in my life," he replied.

"No?" she asked, lifting one eyebrow in an ironic question. "That's odd. The call last night at Mayhew came from his office. You were on the other end. It was a little matter of having stolen the 'evidence' that was under discussion. Meeting at the park, mailing the specifications to keep them safe. And of course the bribe, Wainwright's reward for faithful service." She tilted her head and gave him a knowing look.

He studied her for a moment, while indecision played on his face. She had thought he'd be angry or frightened, but he just looked confused. "Well?" she asked sharply.

"You conned me once. Don't push your luck." His eyes raked over her slowly, from head to toe. He shook his head and slowly walked out of the bedroom.

She waited to hear him leave the apartment, but after a moment's silence she thought he must have left noiselessly, and went into her living room. Tony was standing gazing at the havoc he had wrought. With one toe, he pushed the head of the broken statuette, which rolled over silently. He was looking at it so intently he didn't realize she was there, watching him. Noticing the change in his posture, the weary droop of those proud shoulders, and the haggard lines that had formed on his face, Jerri felt an urge to go to him.

He seemed to sense her presence, for he suddenly turned his head and looked at her. Then the anger returned. His neck stiffened, and he said coldly, "I suggest you not leave town, Miss Tobin. The authorities will want to speak to you."

There were a dozen questions she wanted to ask. Why did he keep asking if she was working with Wainwright? Why would he go to the police, when his crime was so much greater than her own? All she'd done was enter his hotel room and take the envelope. But something in his expression prevented her from speaking at all. He gave one last look and walked away through the ransacked living room, out the door with the broken lock hanging uselessly on its hinges, and down the stairs, with the envelope tucked under his arm. Jerri went to the sofa, picked up a cushion, and sat down.

She felt she ought to be phoning the police, or Elsa Mayhew, or someone, but confusion held her immobile. If Wainwright wasn't working with Tony . . . but he was. The call to Tony had come from his office. Unless someone else in the engineering department was using Wainwright's phone . . . Nancy had said they left that line plugged in, and the other engineers used it. But who? Could it have been Nick Charleston? She'd never heard either Nick or Wainwright speak, and couldn't be certain whose voice it was. In the park, too, it had been so dark she'd only seen a tall form. Nick was tall . . .

But they'd spoken on the phone of evidence and rewards. Of course the innocent needed evidence, too, to prove guilt on the other party's part. And maybe Nick was in line for promotion after helping on this job. Tony had said he was sending in a bright young man, someone who obviously would be moving up quickly in the organization.

She felt weak and chastened with the possibility that she'd been so wrong about Tony. Why hadn't she stopped to consider other possibilities? Everything he had told her previously tallied with this new interpretation. If someone —Wainwright apparently—had changed the specs to destroy the motors, then of course Tony needed evidence to prove it. The precaution of not wanting to be seen with Nick that night must have been done to keep Wainwright from becoming suspicious. If he had noticed the evidence was gone, he might easily suspect the newest employee, and follow him.

And if all this conjecture was true, then Tony wasn't what she had feared and despised. He was just a smart businessman doing his job. He wasn't a criminal after all. Her heart lifted with the knowledge. It had been like a festering wound, but now it was all right. Everything would be all right. Tony had his evidence, and steps would be taken to set Mayhew back on its feet. Tony's only crime was one small lie—that Wainwright was innocent, and that had been done to protect her, to keep her away from danger, she supposed. Wainwright would be put in prison, Tony would buy Mayhew, and . . .

And leave Leamington. A feeling of desolation crept over her. He wouldn't even come to say good-bye. She wasn't too worried about the police. She had good relations with them and could convince them it was a misunderstanding. Croft would razz her, of course, but that didn't matter. She didn't think Tony would actually sue her for breaking into his hotel room, but he would loathe her for it. She'd lied about being sick last night, and he had sent her the beautiful roses—roses she'd never even seen. She'd not only mistrusted him, but had impulsively thrust herself into his affairs, making difficulties for him. She'd misinterpreted everything. She was an idiot. Nobody could love an idiot.

She looked around at the chaos of her apartment, half-glad to have such a monumental task on her hands. It helped to keep her distracted. It was only mindless physical work, but at least it gave some release to her frustration. She'd have to get the chain and lock fixed, too. That lock had never been any good. She called the locksmith herself rather than report the incident to the landlord.

Waiting for the locksmith gave her a good excuse to stay home. She really couldn't face anything today. She felt too ineffectual, too demoralized. Who'd ever hire a private investigator who was an idiot? Throughout that long morning and afternoon, Jerri kept looking wistfully at the silent phone. Even the police ignored her, though she should be grateful for that. The only person who came was the locksmith. And the only time the phone was used was when she called Mayhew to resign.

At four o'clock she actually felt ill, and sat down to stare dejectedly out the window. It was a warm day. Maybe a soft drink would help. That's when she remembered she hadn't eaten a single bite all day long, not even breakfast in the morning. She should go out and buy a hamburger. Anything to keep busy, to keep at bay the desolating knowledge that she'd ruined everything.

Chapter Ten

Jerri forced herself to go out and order a hamburger, but found no pleasure in the excursion. She took one bite of her food and realized she couldn't swallow it. The milkshake was too thick; it was too much of an effort to draw it through the straw. She ate two chips, then bundled the whole meal into its container and threw it into the garbage. It was still bright out, much too early to go to her apartment and face the interminable evening alone. The office would only remind her that Joe was gone.

She didn't especially want to see Dorothy, but some masochistic corner of her heart wanted to see those roses, so Jerri turned her car toward Seigniory Drive. Her aunt was having a rare night at home without company, but this was a mixed blessing. The phone rang constantly. It seemed Elsa Mayhew had suddenly canceled a party, and her disappointed guests were phoning Dorothy to learn the reason.

While Jerri stared disconsolately at the beautiful bouquet of pink and white roses, the buds opening now and forming a lovely centerpiece in Dorothy's living room, she couldn't help but overhear her aunt on the phone.

"Yes, there's joy in Leamington tonight! Dear Elsa has finally unloaded her bothersome company," Dorothy said excitedly. "Mr. Lupino, the big steel magnate, bought it, you know. And you'll never guess what! George Wainwright has been arrested! He's been doing something illegal to botch up a motor or something, and Mr. Lupino sent in an undercover engineer, just like a James Bond movie, and he stole away the evidence. He's with Elsa right this minute, working out the details of the sale."

Maybe she could take one of the roses without arousing suspicion. Jerri wanted to have one to press for a reminder of this part of her life. She'd thrown out all her teenage mementos when she moved to the States. It was time to start a new memory chest. Dorothy's caller finally hung up and Dorothy came back to the sofa, making it impossible to steal the rose.

Jerri was afraid her aunt would question her about her own part in the affair, but not a word was said about it. Tony must not have told anyone, then. Elsa would certainly have told Dorothy, who would just as certainly have demanded an explanation from her niece.

All Dorothy said was, "And what have you been doing with yourself, Jerri? Have you made it up with your mysterious Anthony?"

"No, that's all over," Jerri said, trying to smile.

"Oh, dear, there's the phone again. That'll be Marg Calder. She's the only one who hasn't called to get the details. Excuse me, I'll be as fast as I can."

This time Jerri wasn't taking any chances. She leaned forward and pulled out one long-stemmed pink rose while Dorothy's back was turned. She protected the head with a tissue, bent the stem, and gently placed the whole thing into her purse. When she tuned in to her aunt's phone conversation, it was the sale of Mayhew that was being discussed again.

"Isn't it exciting?" Dorothy exclaimed. "Oh, no, Mr. Lupino won't be running it himself. He's with Elsa now straightening out a few things. Elsa says he's bringing in one of his own men to do it—Charleston is the name, a bachelor. I have every intention of snaring Mr. Charleston for my niece." She looked over her shoulder and winked at Jerri as she said this.

Jerri smiled dutifully, but she wasn't the least bit interested in Nick Charleston. What was in her mind was that Tony was with Elsa tonight. Would it be all business, or would the meeting end on a different note? A helpless widow, still dangerously attractive, and very much interested in Tony . . .

Tears sprang unbidden to her eyes, and she suddenly knew coming here had been a wretched idea. She had to get out, before she made a complete fool of herself.

Jerri stood up and blew her aunt a kiss. "I have to fly. See you later," she said, and hurried out to her car before Dorothy could hang up and come after her. She drove home and put her rose in water. The new lock on her door was a graphic reminder of the morning.

No wonder Tony had appeared confused at times, and angry. He thought she had been exploiting her father's privileged information for her own gain. She'd figured out that much at least. He thought she was stealing those specifications to either blackmail Wainwright, or to sell them to Tony himself. Some opinion he had of her! She had to admit it must have looked suspicious, her meeting him the instant he set foot in Leamington. At least there was some circumstantial evidence to support his suspicions. What did she really have to go on then? He wore sunglasses and looked too sophisticated for Leamington. Obviously he had been so secretive about everything because he didn't want Wainwright to know he was here, investigating the company.

What a temper he'd been in when he came breaking down her door! It had been more than anger at a conniving, devious woman. It had been anger at someone he had cared about, had trusted. Possibly even loved. But his anger must have simmered down, or she'd have had the police at her door before now. He wasn't going to make any unneeessary trouble for her. That was generous of him. He knew her job required good relations with the police. He probably felt sorry for her, or maybe he just didn't want the bother of a minor court case that would require his returning to Leamington to testify. That was probably it. She really should thank him though, and apologize for her part in the whole debacle.

It was a good enough excuse to phone the hotel, but to no avail. He wasn't in when she called. He was still out at eight o'clock, at nine, at ten. It couldn't possibly take so many hours to settle the business deal. The lawyers would handle the time-consuming details. So Elsa and Tony must be doing something else. They were doing what Tony did so well—making love.

After a restless night in bed, Jerri awoke at seven the next morning, feeling as if she had been beaten with clubs. Her joints ached, her head ached, but most of all, her heart ached. She thought if she could get to the shower without dying, she might feel better. A hot shower followed by a cold rinse brought some semblance of life back to her weary body. Out of custom, she went to the kitchen and lifted down the cereal box, but she found she was only hungry enough to eat half a bowl of corn flakes. This gave her enough energy to go into her bedroom and dress.

Jerri didn't think, at first, why she was choosing her outfit so carefully. She rejected the businesslike suit she had worn the morning before, and she spurned her jeans and slacks. She looked over her clothes till she spotted a youthful cotton dress of pale blue, with a white collar. She brushed her hair out loose and caught it back with a blue hair band. Alice in Wonderland popped into her head when she stood back and surveyed herself in the mirror. So that's what her subconscious was up to! She was going to show Tony Lupino what an innocent young thing she was, and make him feel sorry for having abused her. She was vexed with herself for such scheming, even if it was her subconscious that was to blame. Of course she'd change, now that her ego knew what she was up to. Or would she? All's fair in love and war, she decided, and ventured forth in her blue dress and hair band.

As she drove to the Everett, she planned the meeting. She'd begin with an apology for her mistake, and thank him for not calling the police. That was a beginning at least.

She'd ask if there was anything she could do to make up for the trouble she'd caused him—drive him to the airport, perhaps. That would be a thoughtful gesture, and redolent with memories, if the man had a heart at all.

She arrived at the Everett at eight, but was afraid of approaching the desk, in case she should be recognized from the morning before. The Everett might be less considerate than Tony in the matter of pressing charges. She decided to go to the coffee shop and wait for him there. He'd eaten breakfast here yesterday, so presumably that was his practice.

She picked up the morning paper and positioned herself with a view of the door. While waiting, she read an article about Lupino's purchase of the Mayhew Company. A careful perusal of the four columns showed her that her name had been suppressed, and that Tony had been doing exactly what he had told her with regard to buying the company. There was no suggestion of anything underhanded, but rather high praise for his acumen. When her coffee arrived, she set aside the paper. Just as she picked up her cup, she saw the unmistakable form of Tony Lupino coming toward the glass door.

He was wearing the light suit and dark shirt he'd worn the day he arrived. The only difference was that he didn't have on his dark glasses. He hadn't seen her, which allowed her to study him as he drew nearer. How had her mind transformed this respectable businessman into a criminal? Circumstantial evidence, a vivid imagination, and a mistrust of the power of his appeal.

He walked past without noticing her. She cleared her throat and called, "Tony!" in a high, unnatural voice.

He turned around and, when he saw her, froze in his

tracks. She thought he wasn't going to speak to her. There was an air of cool reserve about him that caused her resolution to weaken. If he didn't stop, if he didn't voluntarily come and sit down, she wouldn't have the nerve to force the issue. His dark eyes didn't look like liquid today; they had frozen to cold, black obsidian.

"Good morning," he said, without approaching the table, but at least he spoke, and didn't walk away.

"I'd like to buy you breakfast," she said, forcing a smile on her face.

Seeing his indecision, the reluctance to come to her, she rushed on. "I recommend the eggs Benedict."

There was one awful instant when she was sure he was going to walk away. He examined her coolly, with a mocking look at her childish outfit, but finally he took a step toward her and sat down. The wisp of hope that still survived in her grew stronger.

"What brings you here?" he asked, but he looked supremely uninterested in the answer.

It was impossible to be humble and sincere and all the things she had planned to be, when he spoke so gruffly. She tried for brightness instead. "I was warned not to leave town. A woman has to eat," she answered.

"Woman? I thought you were posing as a child today," he mocked. "If that pinafore and hair ribbon were donned for the purpose of softening me up, I should inform you, I'm unmoved."

An embarrassed flush crept up her neck. "I just grabbed the first thing in my closet," she said. "I didn't want to miss you." Her voice was low, with all the former brightness dulled to humility. She bent her head over the menu to hide her embarrassment.

For a moment Tony stared at the top of her head, then he reached for a menu, too. "The eggs Benedict, you recommended, wasn't it? I was sure an Egg McMuffin would be your preference."

She looked up and saw a reluctant smile tugging at the corners of his lips and was encouraged. "Well, the eggs Benedict are something like it, only they'll probably ruin it with gooey hollandaise sauce."

"Which you recommend so highly!" he inserted, lifting an eyebrow. His smile didn't widen, but the eyes were defrosting.

She rushed in to take advantage of it. "Tony, I'm sorry. It's just that when I heard Nick calling from Wainwright's office, and talking to you about the evidence and reward, and about this deal being so profitable, I thought . . ."

"I know what you thought!" he said, swift anger flaring again. "A flattering assessment of my character!"

But even angry emotions were better than that awful chill. Angry emotions could be turned around. It was indifference that was so hard to manage. "You must admit the switchboard was a stupid place to have put me! How was I supposed to find out anything, stuck behind a switchboard all day long? I thought you'd done it on purpose to keep me harmlessly occupied."

"I did! Nick was there to do the job. I didn't want you getting in his way. Nick had the keys to Wainwright's office and private files. He knew exactly what he was looking for."

She was hurt that he hadn't trusted her competence. Her lips turned down, and she bit her underlip to hold it steady.

"I just didn't want you to get hurt," he admitted gruffly.

The waitress came, but since Tony only ordered toast and coffee, Jerri ordered the same. She firmed her resolution to forge on with her apology. "It was good of you not to report me to the police," she said, after the waitress left. "At least I guess you didn't, since I haven't heard from them."

"I assume you didn't report me either?" he asked. "I half expected a bill for cleaning your apartment and breaking your door."

"That's all right. I got everything fixed up."

"If that little statue I broke was valuable, I'll replace it," he said, but in a careless way.

"Don't worry about it."

The apology and thanks were out of the way. If she meant to take any more positive step toward friendship, this was the time, but her courage had dissipated. It wasn't easy to pitch yourself at a man like Tony. He didn't seem to be in the mood. He was preoccupied, unhappily so.

He sat rubbing his chin, with a faraway, thoughtful look in his eyes. "I owe you an apology, too," he admitted. "I thought you were either giving Wainwright a hand, or planning to sell the specifications to him. They're the only concrete evidence we have against him. I couldn't imagine any other reason why you took them."

"I don't even know Wainwright. I thought he was the man who met you at the wharf."

"At the wharf? You were there, too?" Tony exclaimed, his eyes widening.

"When I heard him talking to you on the phone, naturally I had to go and try to overhear what you said," she answered reasonably.

"But why? What did it have to do with *you?* Nobody was paying you for investigating this case." He stared at her in confusion.

"No, but it was Joe's case in the first place. He never got a chance to see it through," she added.

"I'd forgotten the young can be so naive and idealistic," he said, shaking his head. "Where did you hide? Behind the statue?"

"In the bushes. I didn't hear a thing," she admitted.

"That's a dangerous profession you've gotten yourself into, Jerri," he cautioned. "If it *had* been Wainwright, you might have found yourself—" He stopped short and lifted his shoulders. "Well, who knows? He's a desperate man, and a lot was riding on his scheme. He planned to force the company to its knees, and buy it dirt cheap. Then, of course, the faulty motor would be fixed and business would go on briskly."

"I don't suppose he would have killed me," she countered, but she knew it wasn't impossible. She could be a corpse in the morgue now, and for what? She hadn't even been officially on the case. After all her work, she wasn't going to make a penny. She wouldn't even be getting any thanks. She'd been nothing but a nuisance.

The toast arrived and Tony began spreading marmalade in a distracted way. He didn't warn her of the danger again, didn't try to talk her out of her job, as the people who loved her were always doing. Dad and Dorothy and Mike McCane. And Tony, too, earlier, when he cared for her. Obviously he didn't care for her now.

"I guess you'll be leaving town pretty soon, huh?" she asked.

"The lawyers are working out details with Elsa today.

They'll be returning to New York this afternoon. I want to run out and see Bill Dallyn again before I go. I'd like to hire him as a consultant for a year or so. I hope to get away early this evening on the charter flight," he answered calmly.

"It leaves at seven," she said automatically. At seven o'clock tonight Tony would be leaving, just as he had come. This could be her last time with him, and she couldn't think of anything to say.

"I see you're not hacking your cab today. Have you got a case on?" he inquired.

"I'm just on my way to the office. I have to check with an associate in New York," she invented quickly, hoping to give the impression she was doing well.

"That's too bad. I hoped you might drive me to Glen Williams again," he said.

"Oh, I wouldn't mind! I'll drive you in my own car," she offered at once.

"No, no, I wouldn't dream of interfering in your business. Actually I'll probably be there for hours. It was thoughtless of me to suggest it," he said, in rather a final way.

"Maybe the next time you're in town," she suggested. "You will be back, I suppose?" *Please let him say yes. Let him say he'll call me.*

"Oh, yes, I'll be in and out of town for a month or so, till Nick gets things running smoothly," he answered offhandedly.

"Perhaps I'll see you then. If you need a cab, I mean," she added, as he didn't leap on the suggestion.

"You're the first one I'll call if I need a lift," he said, but nonchalantly, with no overtones of reconciliation. Then he bit into his toast.

She sat indecisive, trying to work up her courage to continue. "Or even if you *don't* need a lift," she offered. There, she couldn't say much more without being positively pushy.

"Yes, I'll bear in mind your other occupation as well, but really I don't expect to need a private investigator."

She heard this with falling hopes. It didn't occur to him to look her up on anything but business.

"You never know," was all she could say.

"That's true. Life is full of surprises. If anyone had told me half an hour ago that I'd be talking to you today without physical violence, I'd have had him locked up. I'm glad we had this talk, Jerri. You didn't really have to don your disguise to bring me under your thumb, you know. In fact, I think I preferred you in the Paris gown. Or even your jeans," he added. "Good lord, look at the time!" he exclaimed suddenly, and leaped up. "I was supposed to be meeting my staff five minutes ago. Will you excuse me? Thanks for breakfast, Jerri."

"You're welcome," she replied dully. He hadn't called her Geraldine once. All he could think of was business.

Tony leaned over her before leaving. He was smiling an enigmatic little smile, as his eyes lingered on her face. "When we were discussing my preferred outfit a moment ago, I forgot to mention your cap. It definitely becomes you. Humility doesn't. Forget it, Jerri. You didn't make as big an ass of yourself as I did, and I'm old enough to know better."

"Let's call it even," she said.

"Even? I'm not satisfied with even. I usually get the better of my opponents, Geraldine." He patted her shoulder as though she were a child, and left.

She ate her toast desultorily, paid the bill, and left. He'd called her Geraldine, for what that was worth.

Jerri drove to her office. There was nothing interesting in the mail and no clients on the recording machine. She phoned a couple of store managers her father had been trying to sell an electronics system to, and they both said they'd think about it and call her later. They'd been saying that for months. She took out her book on electronics and yawned over the incomprehensible and utterly boring devices she was trying to sell.

When the phone rang at eleven-thirty, she was jarred from a reverie that had nothing to do with circuits. "Jerri, it's Mike. Are you free today? Josh's wife is coming home from the hospital. He booked off. I've got a cab with no driver, starting at two this afternoon."

"I'm free," she said, happy to be reprieved from sitting in her quiet office, where the dust was slowly settling around her.

After cleaning up her office, she went home to change into her plaid shirt, jeans, leather vest, and her tan boots that were so comfortable.

It was good to have people to talk to, places to go, even if they were other people's places. She had to go to the Everett Hotel twice, and though she didn't see any sign of Tony either time, it added a little something to her day.

She picked up a submarine sandwich and coffee at six-fifteen and drove the cab to the taxi yard to eat in peace. What am I doing here? she asked herself. I speak three languages fluently. I have the five thousand from Joe in the bank, but not a single job prospect. Am I going to spend the rest of my life driving cabs, and tracking down errant husbands?

Her father had got all the security accounts a town this size offered. If she were going to stay in the business, she'd have to leave Leamington and go to a bigger city. Should she think of going to work for a travel agency? She didn't want to be a tour guide, and she didn't want to sit behind a desk selling tickets and arranging trips either. What *did* she want? As if she didn't know! She wanted Tony Lupino, but he didn't want her.

Chapter Eleven

Jerri had just taken one bite from her sandwich when the dispatcher's voice came whining forth from the taxi radio.

"Pickup at the Everett. Number four take it," the dispatcher said.

Jerri looked at her watch. It was six-thirty. Tony's plane left at seven. It might be him leaving the hotel. She switched her radio on to transmit and said, "I'd like to take that Everett pickup."

"Number four is in the vicinity," the dispatcher replied.

"Please! It's important!" Jerri said, her voice urgent.

"The pickup has to meet a plane. Better let four take it."

"I'm taking it. I'm leaving right now," Jerri said firmly, and set down her sandwich. She turned the key, threw the car into reverse, and squealed out of the yard.

She drove like a demon through town, streaking through

yellow lights. At one point she found herself going the wrong way on a one-way street, but fortunately there was no other traffic, and no policeman to catch her. Jerri was afraid car four would beat her to the Everett. Her heart throbbed painfully as she sped along the road, saying a silent prayer that she'd get there first.

She hardly dared hope anything more would come from it than another short look at Tony, but she had to make the attempt. Their relationship had begun in this very cab. In fact, her happiest memories of him were centered around this dusty vehicle. And he'd said he liked her best in her cap, too.

She had taken off her cap to eat, but she lifted it from the seat now and cocked it at a rakish angle over her eye before she got out at the hotel. Her heart leaped when she saw that Tony was waiting in the lobby with his luggage. The doorman carried the large bag, and Jerri darted forward to relieve Tony of his briefcase and the smaller suit bag.

A smile lit Tony's face when he recognized her. If nothing else happened, that smile alone was worth the reckless dash to the hotel. Jerri beamed back. "Take your bags, sir?"

He handed them over, and while she put them in the trunk, he opened the front door and got in. When Jerri joined him a moment later, he'd taken her coffee from the rack and was sipping it.

"The airport, I believe?" she asked, putting the car in gear.

"No wonder I couldn't reach you at the office. I've been calling ever since I got back from visiting Dallyn," he said.

"Really?" There was a trembling excitement rising in

her. When she spoke, her breath was short. "What were you calling me for?"

"What do you think, Geraldine?" he asked in that insinuating purr that caused her pulse to race. He reached over and removed her cap and placed it on his own head. The rays of the setting sun slanted through the windshield making vision difficult. Tony drew out his sunglasses and put them on.

"If you're stealing my hat, you better let me have the shades. I can't see a thing. The peak keeps the sun out of my eyes," she said, squinting through the window.

"You take the shades. I want to see your hair," he replied, and handed her the dark glasses. "It reminds me of the princesses from fairytales. They usually had hair like spun gold. Rapunzel, Cinderella, all of them."

It was very hard to concentrate on driving with his fingers fondling her hair, rolling it around his fingers. "Not Snow White. She had black hair," she replied, her voice quivering.

"Yes, and look what she attracted—a gang of dwarfs."

She pushed his hand away. "I have a sensitive scalp. That hurts," she said, but it was the tumult of feelings that was bothering her.

"A little suffering is good for the soul. You put *me* through hell," he countered, giving a curl a little tug before letting go. He crossed his arms on his chest, glared into the sun and said firmly, "This has got to stop, Geraldine."

"What has to stop?" she asked, intrigued.

He uncrossed his arms and turned to glare at her profile. "I can't work knowing you're mixed up with criminals. My accountant had to go over the new dividend schedule with me three times this afternoon. I kept picturing you skulking in the dark behind those bushes.'' As he spoke, she felt warm fingers stroking the nape of her neck.

"But it was broad daylight this afternoon, and I wasn't skulking. I was driving the cab for Mike.''

"That's another thing! I never know where you are. You mentioned doing a job for your New York associate,'' he complained. "Those runaway husband cases can be dangerous. They could turn nasty on you in a flash. Men in that position are angry and frustrated.''

"It's too bad you were worried, Tony. I haven't had a case all day,'' she admitted.

"Driving a cab has its dangers, too,'' he pointed out.

A bubble of joyous laughter rose up, but she bit it back. He *did* care! "Especially when your fare sits in the front seat and fondles your neck!'' she answered. "Do you have your ticket for the plane?''

"I don't need one. The flight was full, and I had to charter a private plane. That was your fault, too!'' he charged. "I sat on the fence so long trying to decide what to do about you that the plane was full by the time I phoned. I used to be a firm, decisive man, making important decisions in a minute.''

"You don't have to do anything about me,'' she pointed out reasonably. "I'm not your problem.''

He glared harder than before and said, "I've made you my problem.''

"Another takeover, huh?'' she asked. Finally the laughter bubbled up. She couldn't control it any longer.

"I can't allow you to spend your nights chasing criminals and dogs. Dogs can be vicious, too. There's rabies around this time of the year," he warned. "And I wish you'd stop laughing at me!"

"Then stop being so ridiculous! You're worse than Dorothy and Mike combined," she complained, but tolerantly. She knew it was concern that gave rise to these complaints. "Maybe I better stick to having alarm systems installed. Of course there's always the danger of electrocution," she added jokingly. "Some of them have wicked currents of 110 volts."

"If you were standing in water at the time, it could be hazardous," Tony insisted stubbornly.

"Crossing the street can be hazardous," she pointed out. "You seem to have developed a very tender regard for my safety since this morning." She took a quick glance while she drove, and was gratified to see no laughter on his face, but concern.

"I have my pride. I haven't been accused of being a *thief* before. We Latins are a little volatile," he explained.

"We Irish have a touch of temper, too," she reminded him. She decided to pass a truck that was impeding her vision.

"Some of you are terrible drivers as well. The plane isn't going to leave without me, Geraldine. You can slow down to seventy or eighty. Or did you plan to fly us to New York in the taxi?"

"No, just to the airport."

"Slow down or you'll pass it," he said, as the airfield came into view before them.

She turned in at the airport road and drew into the parking lot. They were out of the sun's glare now, and she removed the glasses. A small plane was waiting on the runway. It was six forty-five. "That must be your plane," Jerri said, and looked hopefully for some more substantial statement of his feelings before he left. He removed her cap and set it on the seat.

"Very likely," he agreed. His eyes never left her face. "I can see you're eager to be rid of me, but first we have to decide what to do about you." As he spoke, he slid along the seat and put his arm around her shoulder.

"I don't care to have my life arranged in two minutes, especially by someone other than myself," she told him calmly.

"*Ourselves*, Geraldine," he modified. "The takeover, remember? Call it a merger if you prefer." His head descended to hers in a maddeningly slow fall.

"But we're not *us*. We're just you and me," she whispered, gazing into his eyes.

As his lips brushed her cheek, he said softly, "We'll get a proper contract drawn up." His lips settled gently on hers, and a serene peace surrounded them.

Ourselves. Us. The words echoed warmly in her mind, bringing a sense of fullness, of having found a special someone to belong to, and to belong to her. His arms were around her, crushing her against him and his lips moved hungrily. She felt already as if they were one. Certainly she would feel as if a part of her would be torn from her when he climbed on that plane and left. She held him tightly, with a sense of urgency at the knowledge that he had to leave. Reluctantly, she loosened her grip.

"The plane's waiting," she pointed out.

"Let it. What's more important, us or a chunk of metal? We have to decide what's to be done about your business. We haven't talked about where we'll live. . . . I know you have strong feelings about Leamington," he said doubt-fully.

"No, my strong feelings about Leamington are buried in St. John's Cemetery. Home is where the heart is. Corny, huh?" she asked.

She expected Tony would be happy to hear this, but a frown deepened on his forehead. "Darling, I really think you should stay in Leamington. It's not that far from New York. I'd be happy to commute—not every day, of course."

She felt her spine stiffen, pulling away from him. "Just what kind of contract did you have in mind, Tony?" she asked. What a fool she'd been!

"A marriage contract!" he answered instantly.

"Then why do you want me to stay in Leamington?"

"Because the criminals are relatively harmless here. I couldn't live knowing you were chasing hardened criminals in the city."

"Oh, is that all!" she exclaimed, and laughed for pure relief. "Well, to tell the truth, I don't have a very active business here. I've been thinking of retiring."

"You're sure?" he asked, but she saw the shadow leave his eyes.

"Tony, I don't have a business at all. What I have is a dusty office and an answering machine that takes Dorothy's calls. And I really hate the 'wave of the future'—electronics. I just came here to be with Dad, and I'm not sorry I did, but now he's gone. My place is with the one I love—*you*," she said softly, stroking his cheek.

A smile of ineffable tenderness glowed on Tony's face. "I'm glad to hear that, Geraldine. I'll make the transition as painless as possible for you. You'll be happy to hear there's a pizza place two blocks from my apartment, and a hot dog vendor passes the door regularly. You'll feel right at home.'' He looked suddenly thoughtful. ''Maybe I'll have better luck in New York finding a shepherdess. I didn't have any here in Leamington. I can't tell you how badly I felt when I broke that delicate little thing.''

Jerri answered lightly to dispel the memory. ''I can glue the head back on. The important thing is that we made up.'' She kissed him softly.

When they broke apart, Tony gazed at her and shook his head. ''Who knows how long it might have taken me to meet you if you hadn't been working with Joe? I suppose we might have met in Europe, but I haven't made a habit of hanging out on the French Riviera.''

''Maybe you should. It would be a nice spot for a honeymoon,'' Jerri suggested.

''Why not?'' Tony grinned teasingly at her. ''France is the fifth largest producer of steel in the world.''

Jerri drew back and eyed him suspiciously. ''Is this going to be a honeymoon or a working trip?''

Instead of answering, Tony drew her back into his arms for a lengthy kiss. When they finally broke apart, Jerri was breathless with longing.

Tony's voice was ragged when he spoke. ''As you can see, Geraldine, since I met you my interest in mergers has changed to the more personal sort.'' He captured her hand and brought it to his lips, then locked his fingers with hers. ''From now on it will be just you and me, in the most beautiful merger ever merged.''

*Fall in love again for the first time
every time you read a Silhouette Romance novel.*

If you enjoyed this book, and you're ready to be carried away by more tender romance...get 4 romance novels FREE when you become a Silhouette Romance home subscriber.

Act now and we'll send you four touching Silhouette Romance novels. They're our gift to introduce you to our convenient home subscription service. Every month, we'll send you six new Silhouette Romance books. Look them over for 15 days. If you keep them, pay just $11.70 for all six. Or return them at no charge.

We'll mail your books to you two full months *before they are available anywhere else*. Plus, with every shipment, you'll receive the Silhouette Books Newsletter absolutely free. *And Silhouette Romance is delivered free.*

Mail the coupon today to get your four free books—and more romance than you ever bargained for.

Silhouette Romance is a service mark and a registered trademark.

------------------ **MAIL COUPON TODAY** ------------------

Silhouette Romance®
120 Brighton Road, P.O. Box 5084, Clifton, N.J. 07015-5084

☐ Yes, please send me FREE and without obligation, 4 exciting Silhouette Romance novels. Unless you hear from me after I receive my 4 FREE books, please send me 6 new books to preview each month. I understand that you will bill me just $1.95 each for a total of $11.70—with no additional shipping, handling or other charges. **There is no minimum number of books that I must buy, and I can cancel anytime I wish.** The first 4 books are mine to keep, even if I never take a single additional book.

☐ Mrs.　☐ Miss　☐ Ms.　☐ Mr.　　　　　　　BRRLL4

Name　　　　　　　　　(please print)

Address　　　　　　　　　　　　　　　　Apt. No.

City　　　　　　　　State　　　　　　Zip
(　　)
Area Code　Telephone Number

Signature (If under 18, parent or guardian must sign.)

This offer, limited to one per household, expires June 30, 1985. Prices and terms subject to change. Your enrollment subject to acceptance by Silhouette Books.

Let Silhouette Inspirations show you a world of Christian love and romance... for 15 days, free.

If you want to read wholesome love stories...with characters whose spiritual values are as meaningful as yours...then you'll want to read Silhouette Inspirations™ novels. You'll experience all of love's conflicts and pleasures—and the joy of happy endings—with people who share your beliefs and goals.

These books are written by Christian authors...Arlene James, Patti Beckman, Debbie Macomber, and more...for Christian readers. Each 192-page volume gives you tender romance with a message of hope and faith...and of course, a happy ending.

We think you'll be so delighted with Silhouette Inspirations, you won't want to miss a single one! We'd like to send you 2 books each month, as soon as they are published, through our Home Subscription Service. Look them over for 15 days, free. If you enjoy them as much as we think you will, pay the enclosed invoice. If not, simply return them and owe nothing.

A world of Christian love and spirituality is waiting for you...in the pages of Silhouette Inspirations novels. Return the coupon today!

Silhouette Inspirations Home Subscription Service
120 Brighton Road, P.O. Box 5084, Clifton, NJ 07015-5084

Yes, I'd like to receive two new Silhouette Inspirations each month as soon as they are published. The books are mine to examine for 15 days, free. If I decide to keep the books, I will pay only $2.25 each, a total of $4.50. If not delighted, I can return them and owe nothing. There is never a charge for this convenient home delivery—no postage, handling, or any other hidden charges. *I understand there is no minimum number of books I must buy, and that I can cancel this arrangement at any time.*

☐ Mrs.   ☐ Miss   ☐ Ms.   ☐ Mr.   BCFLP4

Name _____ (please print) _____

Address _____ Apt # _____

City _____ State _____ Zip _____
(   )
Area Code   Telephone Number

Signature (If under 18, parent or guardian must sign.)

This offer, limited to one per customer, expires June 30, 1985. Terms and prices subject to change. Your enrollment is subject to acceptance by Silhouette Books.

SILHOUETTE INSPIRATIONS is a trademark and service mark.

READERS' COMMENTS ON SILHOUETTE ROMANCES:

"I would like to congratulate you on the most wonderful books I've had the pleasure of reading. They are a tremendous joy to those of us who have yet to meet the man of our dreams. From reading your books I quite truly believe that he will some-day appear before me like a prince!"

—L.L.*, Hollandale, MS

"Your books are great, wholesome fiction, always with an upbeat, happy ending. Thank you."

—M.D., Massena, NY

"My boyfriend always teases me about Silhouette Books. He asks me, how's my love life and natu-rally I say terrific, but I tell him that there is always room for a little more romance from Sil-houette."

—F.N., Ontario, Canada

"I would like to sincerely express my gratitude to you and your staff for bringing the pleasure of your publications to my attention. Your books are well written, mature and very contemporary."

—D.D., Staten Island, NY

*names available on request